The Haunting of Barrington Heights Estates

By

Raylee Anne McKenna

COPYRIGHT

Copyright @ 2021 by
Raylee Anne McKenna

ALL RIGHTS RESERVED. NO part of this book may be reproduced or transmitted in any form by any means, electronic or mechanical, including photocopying and recording, or by any information storage and retrieval system, except as may be expressly permitted in writing from the author.

ISBN: 9798455566929

Printed in the United States of America

rayleeanne@aol.com

Published by: BookMarketeers

Acknowledgements

Since this is a true story, some names have been changed to respectfully protect the individual's privacy.

A special thanks to **South Carolina Paranormal Research and Investigations,** for their dedication and professionalism demonstrated during an incredibly challenging time for our family. The findings from your investigation helped bring us a little closer to the closure we needed as a family.

Thanks again,

Raylee Anne…

Dedication

This book is dedicated to my ***husband*** for his unwavering support during the last 20 + years of marriage.

To my parents, ***West and Mildred***, thank you for the values you so beautifully wove into the fabric of our souls. We have lived by all the examples you have lovingly taught us.

My Favorite Quote

THE ONE YOU FEED

There's a well-known legend about two wolves:

A Cherokee elder was teaching his grandchildren about life.

"A fight is going on inside me," he said to them. "It is a terrible fight, and it is between two wolves. One is evil – he is anger, envy, sorrow, regret, greed, arrogance, self-pity, guilt, resentment, inferiority, lies, false pride, superiority, and ego." He continued, "The other is good – he is joy, peace, love, hope, serenity, humility, kindness, benevolence, empathy, generosity, truth, compassion, and faith. The same fight is going on inside you – and inside every other person too."

The grandchildren thought about it and after a minute one of them asked, **"Which wolf will win***?"*

The elder simply replied.

"The one you feed."

Author Unknown

Book References

THE HAUNTING OF BARRINGTON HEIGHTS ESTATES

These are the direct Links for the evidence on **YouTube**. These are the actual Audio and Video Recordings collected during the Investigation by SCPRAI. Also, the slideshow is from the original security camera pictures. There is also footage taken from the security camera included as well. I recommend listening to each one in a quiet place so you can experience the actual evidence as you follow along in the book.

Keeping the lights on is optional..

Chapter 10. "Hispanic Ghost Party," Audio/ Video. This was caught on the security camera during the same week after my mother had seen the Hispanic spirits in the den.

https://youtu.be/FM0gCHXyB8g

Chapter 12. "Voodoo Ladies," caught on actual security camera footage.

https://youtu.be/R_eOWR1cv2E

Chapter 15. "Peek a Boo!" (Video #1). Raylee Anne's bedroom; also noted as the front bedroom or first bedroom on the investigators' final report. Looks like the spirit gets caught peeking on the team and quickly moves away from the doorway. Haunted closet on the left. That is the closet where Raylee Anne had stored her Ventriloquists Dolls.

They were on the top shelf of that closet and that is where Raylee Anne sees the dolls looking at her through the slats of the bi-folding doors after a spirit had turned on the light in the closet.

https://youtu.be/XOmFsF6B1UA

Chapter 15. "Peeping spirits get caught." (Video #2). **Watch the timeline on both Video #1 and Video #2**. Also, noted is the haunted bathroom mirror where the old lady was seen in the mirror from Chapter 5. Pay close attention to the Orbs too. Also, from Chapter 14, you can see the back of the actual loveseat where the Hispanic female spirit was sitting when she turned around and told my mother, **"I told them you weren't going to be happy about this!"**

https://youtu.be/DDZPxFTf_Mk

Chapter 15. Raylee Anne's bedroom **(Video #3).** Actual investigation video. Look at the Periscope 360 (sitting on the table) as it lights up. This is the *Hotspot* marked on the diagram of the house for the team leader to investigate that location.

https://youtu.be/_ywhUSWWj6s

Chapter 15. Hall View **(Video #4).** More footage from the investigation. Look at the Orbs. Look at the Investigator in the Hallway between the two opened doorways; this is a great video to see my old, haunted bedroom and where the old living room/new formal dining room are located. Also, that's the location of the Malevolent Spirit that warned my mother in the Hall.

Note* The hallway is much longer than it appears in the videos.

https://youtu.be/KhRrJ5yn8Ww

Chapter 15. Audio recording #1- Child spirit speaking, **"There's something on the shelf that can see us."** This was caught on audio while the paranormal team had positioned a camera to face the desk that was in the back corner of the den/living room. The desk has a tall shelf above it. The team also had other equipment used for their investigation sitting on the desk as well.

https://youtu.be/WWzgWwDgvT4

Chapter 15. Audio recording #2 – Female spirit speaking, **"There's something going on!"**

https://youtu.be/3BoGGzSxia0

Chapter 15. Audio recording #3 - Female spirit caught on audio mimicking a team member during a conversation with another member. **"Yeah."**

https://youtu.be/fGLz8Wq-QOg

Chapter 15. Audio recording #4 – (1 of 2 recordings) . **" I want Gangster Boo!'** A female spirits states after the team members were talking about naming the Teddy Bear "Gangster Boo," from the movie Ghost Busters.

https://youtu.be/DNk-iJuDjP4

Chapter 15. Audio recording #4 – (2 of 2 recordings). Audio from the second team member's recording, **"I want**

Gangster Boo!" The female spirit's state after the team member were talking about naming the Teddy Bear Gangster Boo from the movie Ghost Busters.

https://youtu.be/9PR2JLim0CQ

Chapter 15. Audio recording #5 - **Female Humming**. Believed by family members to be some type of residual haunting of their mother; she would *hum* through the entire house all the time. Only one problem though, our mother had moved out weeks before the investigation was even initiated.

https://youtu.be/TRb8WPjserQ

Chapter 15. Audio recording # 6 - Is the voice of another female. The voice was picked up from a recorder placed in the Master Bedroom, "my moms' room." You can hear a female voice say, **"I know."**

https://youtu.be/cf_F1VEflx4

Chapter 15. Audio recording #7- Mimic of team investigator saying **"On."**

https://youtu.be/GAwulRBn2iE

Chapter 15. Audio recording #8 - Spirit caught on audio **Exhaling or Growling**?

https://youtu.be/l6oXs8Hfh0Y

Chapter 15. Audio recording #9 – (1 of 2 recordings) The Malevolent Male Spirit believed to be **"he,"** and the spirit that I believed had tormented my mother. You can clearly hear the spirit saying, **"Of course I have!"**

https://youtu.be/vhg7PAGC6tk

Chapter 15. Audio recording #9 - The Malevolent Spirit Part 2. **" Of course, I have!"** This is a male spirit; you can hear the meter going off after he speaks, which indicates a spirit energy is nearby.

https://youtu.be/SAOWnZVbQxg

Extra Bonus:

Venice October 2011

Time Warp I caught in Venice. We were a few minutes out from St. Mark's Square when I noticed these amazing unworldly lights shining down on the water from the sky; As I took a picture of them, "I did not see any boats at all in the canal," I was only interested in the beams of lights, but I knew there had to be something going on with those lights, because I had never seen anything like that. Boy, was I right! What a treasure! I had it framed, and it hangs on my wall in my home.

https://youtu.be/TDe34pvHc-Q

Overview

Could you fall asleep at night with the lights on?

You may have to after reading the true story about the paranormal haunting of new author Raylee Anne Mckenna. Raylee Anne was only 5 years old when she moved with her family from the city to the new upcoming Barrington Heights community. The prized real estate sold quickly as many families jumped at the chance of owning a piece of this much sought-after property that had been in the Barrington family for a couple of centuries.

But as the Barrington family moved on to another location, they left some of their family secrets behind……

The old Barrington family cemetery, which had burials all the way back to the 1800s' was supposed to be relocated prior to the sale of all the tracts of land. But when a next-door neighbor shows Raylee Anne's father the stacks of old headstones and grave markers, "her young mind tried to process what that really meant." All she knew was something didn't feel right about what she was hearing and seeing.

Raylee Anne was so excited about moving into the new house that her dad had just finished building. She also looked forward to riding her bike and having lots of room to run and play. However, the excitement was short-lived when she started seeing and hearing things that no one else in the family was experiencing.

As Raylee Anne gets more comfortable in their new home, her mother decides it's time for her to move into her own bedroom; but Raylee Anne had always had a bad feeling about that long dimly lit hall, and since her room was located at the other end of the house, she became totally isolated from the comfy safe feeling of being close to her sister Kat and parents' rooms. A decision that would change the life of a little girl forever, as she falls prey to a malevolent spirit that would feed upon her fears and innocents; all while her family slept peacefully in their beds oblivious to the tortures happening at the end of the dark hall.

Raylee Anne finally pleads with her mother not to make her stay in that room anymore, *"since there was something bothering her in there,"* but her mother didn't feel concerned about what Raylee Anne was telling her, *"back then you didn't hear much about the spirit world,"* so she would comfort her then return her to her bed.

A half a century passes, and the already haunted Barrington Heights, once again shows its true colors and devious dark side, when it goes after Raylee Anne's mother Mildred with a vengeance, they threaten to take everything from her, including her life!

…………..Just like our favorite car or truck, our homes have its own personality. Have you ever had someone say, "I just love your house, it's just so homey feeling?" But what happens when you feel like you are the guest in your own home?

And unwanted guest at that! …………………………………..

Table of Contents

The Early Years	*14*
Moving Day Comes to Barrington Heights	*18*
Hidden Family Cemetery	*25*
Paranormal	*32*
This House is Making Me Ill	*41*
Nobody is Leaving This House	*49*
Memories of The Zombie Man	*58*
The Curse	*68*
Sunroom Visitor and A Doppelganger	*76*
Hispanic Ghost Party	*83*
Busy Spirits	*89*
Voodoo Ladies	*94*
They Know Everything We Say	*102*
Just Let Them Have It!	*108*
Time to Investigate	*118*
House For Sale	*128*
My Closing Thoughts	*134*
Copy of The Final Report From The Investigation	*142*

1

The Early Years

There's no place like home, a quote that goes as far back as the 14th century, and for most people, no truer words were ever spoken. But what happens when your home doesn't feel the same about you? That's what happens to the house in Barrington Heights. Where the land held a century or more of secrets, and a New Home, would become a very unwelcomed guest and a disruption to the souls of Barrington Heights.

This is a true story, an exceedingly difficult one to share. Honestly, it has caused so much trauma in my life. I am almost afraid to tell it from the fear of bringing all that negativity and agitation back into my life. I have slept with the lights on while writing this story. My story is considered "TABOO" by many people. Some people feel uncomfortable talking about it because of the fear of judgment or, in the worst scenario, being questioned on their mental condition. Because of this apprehension, many people find it easier to live their entire life in fear and torment rather than speak out. But I want to share my experiences in hopes that it may spare someone a lifetime of anguish.

My name is Raylee Anne, and I am the middle child of 3 girls. I was born in the South in 1962. My older sister *Kat* is 2 years older than me, and baby sister *Dawn* is 5 years and somewhat younger than I, and she was born about 6 months after we had moved to Barrington Heights.

My parents were a beautiful couple. My mother's name was *Mildred Kelly*, a 5'7 tall beauty queen with sparkling blue eyes. She had high cheekbones that "*I would imagine*" she had inherited from the Indian side of her family. I think her creamy smooth fair skin was "*credited from the Irish Kelly*" side of her family. She had a figure like a model and "*BAM*," no wonder she stole my father's heart in a glance.

My Dad's name was *West Owens*. He was 6'5 tall with jet black hair, dark skin, and gorgeous deep dark brown eyes that were so rich in color, you couldn't even see his pupils (absolutely stunning). He had Cherokee Indian in the bloodline, adding that he works outside in the hot sun all day and another "BAM" my mom got her tall, dark, and handsome man.

Both my parents graduated high school, and both were quite intelligent and business savvy. My mom worked at the bank, and my dad was a brick mason and had entrepreneur skills that he learned from his parents and siblings in construction. They married within a few months after my mom had graduated high school and had turned 18. He, just 19, had graduated one year earlier.

My mom told me stories about how they got married, how they started their family and worked hard for everything. She once told me that my dad wanted to start their family right away when they got married. In answer to my dad's desire, my mom told him that she would not have any babies until they had their own home. They were living with his parents after they got married. So, my daddy, with help from his father, got busy building their first starter home. He planned to build a brick home, 2 bedrooms, 1-bathroom, a small kitchen, and a den that added in the charm of a screened-in porch with a cool breeze and one carport. This was the idea of a perfect home for a beautiful couple with a kid or two.

One of the unique things about this property was the exceptionally large pond that surrounded the house. It used to be a lake before the county put in some new roads. From their back yard, they could put in a boat and fish or fish from the bank. When she first moved to the property, my mom said she would come home from work and find many people in her backyard just fishing away. It has been rumored that gypsies used to gather and sing from the bank of the pond on occasions. I could only imagine that it would be a beautiful sound to hear with all the water around and how it would echo throughout the town.

Every now and then, if there had been a lot of rain, the pond would flood the entire backyard, and my mom did not have a clothes dryer, which was considered a luxury back in the day. She had to put on my dad's size 13 boots on and wade out to the clothesline in the deep water in the mornings to hang them and back out in the evening to bring them back in. She never complained, even though she had worked all day at the bank. She was always happy and singing no matter what she was doing.

In 1965 my dad purchased a much larger tract of land with plans to build a much larger home in the future and possibly their forever home. The Barrington family owned an enormous amount of farmland which quite possibly contained over a thousand plus acres. It was large enough to be its own city. The property had been in the family for over two centuries, and just like a lot of large families, the farmland had been passed down through the years to its inheritors.

In 1964, the Barrington family started selling the family land for a little over $10,000 per acre, "that was a lot of money for an acre in the 1960s." Still, it was prime real estate, with a great location close to a historical lake, not to mention an excellent investment. The extra land my dad purchased would also give him the advantage of building on if they needed more space in the future. The land would also provide plenty of room to plant a large garden, which my parents grew up doing. Basically, anything one would want to do, they would have the room to. Unlike the homes in the city, built side by side, row by row.

2

Moving Day Comes to Barrington Heights

In 1967, my father finished building our new ranch-style brick house. Our new house was enormous in comparison to where I had spent my first years of life. It was exciting to have 3 bedrooms and 2 bathrooms. Daddy also built a separate garage at the backside of the property, and he was able to use the same blueprints that he had used to build our first home. Its bungalow boxed shape and 900 square footages were the perfect sizes for a roomy garage.

For a short period of time, I slept with my sister Kat. I guess my parents wanted us to gradually get used to our new home before putting us in our own rooms since we had shared a bedroom at our other house. I was pretty sure my sister Kat was incredibly happy when the day came for her roommate to get the boot. She and her little attitude would have more room now. Besides that, we did not sleep well together, she went to bed with the chickens, while I never wanted to go to bed, and I disturbed her when I got in the bed so late at 9:00 pm. What can I say, "the queen needed her sleep!"

To be honest, I was scared to sleep in my own room. I had become uncomfortable with the long hall for a while, and I felt like someone was following me when I walked down it. I was constantly looking over my shoulder to see who it was. My new bedroom did not have that same comfy feeling Kat's room had. It was further away from my parents' room and Kat's room. My room was at the other end of the hall with the kitchen, and the hall bathroom was much closer to Kat's room than mine. I would have to walk down the long dark hallway with only a tiny night light placed in the only outlet in the hall. I had to pee a lot at night, and the thought of having to get up and walk alone down that dimly lit hallway made me even more nervous that I felt like I had to pee even more.

Straight across from my room was the living room, another one of my least favorite places in the house. I would make my mom close that door every night because I felt scared with it opened, plus the front door was in that room, and someone might try to kidnap me... *LOL*... And since I was so far away from any other living person, they would not even know I was gone until the next morning.

Since we lived on the dead-end of the street, and the only house at the bottom of the hill, it was very dark, I mean Real Dark! My daddy's garage was located on the backside of the property. I always felt uneasy and like someone was watching me even when my daddy was out there working.

However, the garage had a private driveway which gave the impression it was another residence, especially in the daytime. You wouldn't even know there was a building there at night because it was so black with the lights off. You would not have even been able to see your own hand, just pure blackness, even on a moon-lit night. I hated when I was down there, and it got dark outside, and I would run as fast as my little legs would carry me when daddy turned the lights off in his garage. I ran straight for the house, and this might would have been the only time I could outrun my daddy," and" I wasn't about to be left behind… *NO SIR*, definitely not!

On many occasions, while sitting on the front porch, I would look over into the night where daddy's garage and private driveway were located, "*even though I couldn't actually see it in the darkness*," I would start seeing shadows of what looked like a person. These shadows were even darker than the blackness. They looked as though "they/it?" were walking toward me to the point *I was squinting my eyes trying to figure out who was down there or holler out, "who is there?"*

My sister and I played outside most of the time, regardless of the weather or time of year, as TV was minimal with only local channels, so to have fun, we had to use the power of our imagination or find something to do outside. If it rained, "*no problem*," we would put baby powder on our socks and slide up and down the hardwood floors of our long hallway, that kept us entertained for hours as we waited for the rain to stop, and when it did, outside we would go to ride our bikes through the mud puddles, to see who could project the most water from the rear tire. And yes, we would get injured from time to time. Still, it wasn't a big deal because we had "Merthiolate." It fixed everything known to man, "*the miracle product of its time*," every cut and scratch you may get "no worries, Merthiolate will take care of it." However, the pain from the bright orange antiseptic miracle was far worse than the cut itself. Most kids looked like they had been hit with orange paintballs all over their body that would last for weeks, and going to the doctor was for big stuff like a broken bone or if you were half dead or needed stitches. If it didn't fall into those categories, you were probably treated at home with a kiss on the boo-boo and a pat on the head, and an encouraging nudge back outside to where you got hurt in the first place.

The new elementary school was about to open its doors for the first time and register new students for grades 1 thru 5. The school was built on some of the property purchased from the Barrington family estate too. I think the new school was another reason why so many families moved to this area. Still, since we lived less than one mile from our new school, the district would not be providing school bus transportation, so, our mom would have to take and pick us up every day after school.

My sister and I would be 2 of the many children to christen its halls, and "*until recently, that school had withstood over 5 decades and a couple of generations of"* the first day of school." Kat would be starting the third grade, so she knew what was coming, plus she was a lot more outgoing than I was. She was a tough girl with an attitude to match, and not to mention" the queen of the eye roll," you know the firstborn thinks they are in charge of everything, and *"not knowing any better"*, I thought she was... *LOL*...

Part of the school registration process required getting caught up on your vaccinations, *"you didn't have a choice about being vaccinated in those days, your parents couldn't say."* Well, I just do not think I am going to give my kids these shots", no options there. To get this done before school started, we had to go to my sister Kat's old school, and I knew getting out of the car that morning, this wasn't going to be a good day, and, oh boy, was I right! The nurses immediately started lining us up like cattle, shoulder to shoulder, in a cold cafeteria and vaccinated each of us, one after another, without stopping until they finished that row of children, this by far had to be the most painful shot *EVER*!!! The loud sound of the air gun combined with the echo of all the children crying had paralyzed most of us with fear, and poor little Timmy Brown passed out on the hard cafeteria floor. The nurse just slid him over and kept on with the injections until all the children were physically and mentally scarred for life by the penny-sized reminder branded in our upper arm.

Being only five and not emotionally ready to be away from my family, "just as many of us who started school in June of that year, and then celebrated a late September or

October birthday." Plus, add in the fact that I had never been to kindergarten, "there wasn't many of those around in 1967." I struggled to learn all this new stuff, so I was not a fan right away.

We had settled in, and picking up pinecones from all the pine trees, "*of which there were many,*" became a new and unwelcome chore that had to be done as well as raking all the pine straw created from the monster size trees. There was, however, an interesting oddity on the backside of our property line though. How many people can say that they had an old train in their backyard? It was a red caboose and what I would say was an Orange yellowish engine car. How did this colossal thing get here? There were not any tracks around, and the closest tracks had been many miles away. Still being young and adventurous, my parents had gone with Kat and me to explore it a couple of times. It was old and rusty with pockets of standing smelly water that added to the eerie feeling. Still, it was fascinating at the same time. The train remained there may be a few years before it was moved away, and to this day is a total mystery.

The train was not the only strange part of this mysterious Barrington Heights property. I was riding my bike just like I did almost every day. Up the steep driveway, pedal, pedal, pedal, up the steep dirt hill of Gavon Lane. *"You know the pedaling you have to stand up to do in order to get up a difficult hill?"* I passed Mr. Benny's driveway, then I turned at the top of the hill to the right onto Kate Street, then pedaled down the street about ¾ way, to where the dirt road portion ended. There was a heavily wooded area after Kate Street ended; when something grabbed my attention in the Sky off to my right, it was a giant airplane, "what we would consider a jet today. It was utterly still, and it just hovered just above the tall pine trees in a wooded area that was only about 30 yards from where I stood holding my bike between the legs. It was painted in two colors. I would compare the shade of blue to the color royal blue on the bottom and white on the top. I knew even in my young mind that this was like nothing I had ever seen before. How could this plane just be still in midair? I stared for what seemed like forever when I noticed an older woman looking back at me from the plane's window. She had black shoulder-length hair styled with what I could best describe as a tease to it. She was just staring at me. I do not remember seeing the back or the tail of the airplane. It was just the nose of the plane, to about where the wings should be on a large airplane. I never heard any sounds or recall any engine noise; it was just there. Within a blink of an eye, the plane darted off, and then nothing.

I was baffled at what I had seen and turned my bike around and pedaled as fast as I could back home. I talked excitedly as I told my mom what I had seen and tried to explain to her all the details as she listened. She really did not say much. I knew what I had seen, and the world was starting to make less and less sense to me.

3

Hidden Family Cemetery

There were only a few tracks of land available in our neighborhood, and one of them happened to be right next to our house. It had lots of sand and grass. Occasionally, on a Saturday, many neighbors would bring their children and have a good old fashion baseball game. I remember those games fondly.

The dirt roads offered another great place to play outdoor games. The dirt road was a perfect place to play hotch scotch, tug of war, or just break off a stick from a bush and draw pictures in the sand. Living at the bottom of a steep dead-end road did have its advantages and provided a haven from traffic. And with my mom's, "birds eyes view from the kitchen window," she could keep a watchful eye on us.

Our family was the only one that used that portion of the road except for the Stephens family. They had purchased a large tract of land situated at the back end of the new subdivision, with property lines that backed up to another parcel of land in the neighborhood, including ours, Mr. Benny's, and the Parks family. This section of land was Barrington Heights' most sought out parcel of property, not only because of its size, but its accessibility to three different roads. One of them went to their house while another went to the stables, so they just put a gate on our street, and on a rare occasion, would come through, just to keep the car path from becoming unpassable.

Stephen's home was a unique modern style bi-level that was far ahead of its time. They built the house upon the hillside of the property and painted it in a rich dark brown. With the help of the tall pines that surrounded the house, "nature had created the perfect camouflage, "and the house seemed to blend effortlessly into its surrounding. I did get invited once to come look inside, I knew it would not look like our house, and I was right! It was filled with all kinds of art on the wall and unusual furniture and décor.

I liked Mr. and Mrs. Stephens. They were friendly people. They had three children, two daughters, the older one was named Sarah Beth, and JoJo was the youngest, and a son named Taylor. Their children were about 5 to 10 years older than Kat and me, so we did not see them very often unless they were out riding the horses. We would love it when they would let us pet Thumper and Rebel. One day they even took me for a horseback ride. I thought I was something else, nobody could tell me anything.

Our front porch was so pretty. My Dad had some type of broken, *"what I called"* clay pots mixed in with concrete for the porch's flooring, and with the tall columns, it looked like a grand entrance. The front of our house faced the dirt road of Gavon Lane and the partially fenced backyard at Mr. Benny's house.

Mr. Benny had a large Ranch style house, with a separate oversized garage in the backyard. I do not remember any cars being in there, but he did store his tractor and gardening tools inside. He had a green thumb, too, and always had the most fantastic garden. Corn was his specialty, with stalks so high they look like trees. There were so many corn stalks that you could hardly see through them. He was a generous man who would often share his harvest of a variety of fresh vegetables with our family, as well as the other neighbors. Mr. Benny and his wife were much older than my parents and were simply good ole fashion Christian folk. Mr. Benny would let the kids in the neighborhood play in their yard. Even though their children were grown and gone, they would let us run around and around their house playing chase and hide and go seek while they enjoyed our laughter. They would not let us play around the area behind the garage where the garden was planted. However, that would have been an ideal place for playing hide and go seek. We would have been able to hide in the corn maze for a long time.

One afternoon, in late spring, I heard him at the fence in his garden. He calls out to my mother, "Hi Mildred, he said, how are y'all doing?" "We are doing good Mr. Benny; how about y'all?" Good, Good, he replied. Mom said,

"Your garden is looking so good." He replied, "Yeah, yeah, it is. Walk on over, and we will get you some veggies together, we love homemade veggie soup, so we were always happy to hear that." Mom answered back, "that would be great! Let me run in the house and get my basket." We always had baskets around to pick the beans from our own garden, and of course, I was thrilled because I would get to go into that forbidden cornfield.

After walking around the garden while my mom and Mr. Benny talked, I noticed his fence went deeper into a wooded area than it appeared from our side of the fence, so I followed along the fence line when I realized that the garden area was surrounded by a perfectly shaped triangle fence, so I started walking over to the spot where Mr. Benny had called out to my mother earlier. I peeked over the fence post. It was so weird to be looking down at our house. I remembered how strange it felt and how high up his property seemed. It was almost like I was on a mountain top. Still, in reality, it was only about 2 to 3 feet higher than where the road was. I started feeling disoriented and confused looking over at our house, and I tried to make sense of all the feelings in my little mind. I was so glad when we left there, that feeling that we adults would call "fight or flight," Well, I was in flight mode for sure! And after that day, I never looked at his garden in the same way again. It caused me to be anxious and fearful, with a sense of dread to even look at it, but it was one of the first things you see when walking out the front door of our house, so it was unavoidable.

Haunting of Barrington Heights Estates

It was a fabulous afternoon, and I was watching daddy as he lay brick on our new backyard grill when I heard Mr. Benny hollow over to my dad, "hey West, got a minute? Yes, sir, I do. What can I help you with? Mr. Benny hollers back, "I want to show you something," Sure, I will be right over. I followed behind my dad as we walked up the hill. I watched as Mr. Benny headed toward his garage in the backyard, I felt safe with daddy, but I still was not going in that garden area again.

Mr. Benny kneeled beside the side door of his garage. My Dad kneeled beside him. Mr. Benny started talking about the oblong stone blocks that were loosely stacked at their feet and the other stone blocks that had a rounded top leaning against the side of the garage. As I listened to his story, I heard things that a child should not have heard and would haunt my little mind. Mr. Benny said, "well West, you see, (his eyes gazing up at the fenced-in area, lifting his hand and pointing his finger back and forth at the entire width of the garden area behind his garage. This area was used as the cemetery of the Barrington family, with lineages all the way back to the 1800s." After the older family members had passed away, many of the kinfolks had sold this tract of land and had all the graves relocated. These are the headstones and grave markers that were left behind. My Dad, a very superstitious man, "a family-taught thing that gets passed down from one generation to another generation. And God help you if you break with protocol. It was serious business with a Cherokee Bloodline. And do not let a Black Cat cross your path, especially while driving. That was JU JU bad luck. You better lick that pointing finger and X that out on your windshield

Haunting of Barrington Heights Estates

immediately. My Dad had so many X's across every car or truck he had or ever owned, for that matter. And when the sun would hit the X's precisely right, you could see every one of them, and no matter how many times you wiped them or used window cleaner, nothing would ever remove them.

Mr. Benny said, "some of these blocks looked to be in surprisingly good shape. You could use them in the grill you are building." My Dad responded, "yeah, that's true, I will take a couple off your hands then," I could tell that my dad really didn't want to take them, but didn't want to hurt Mr. Benny's feelings either, so my dad reached down and picked up a couple, they were heavy. They had to be carried with both arms extended out. Mr. Benny, however, thought daddy could make use of more than a couple and proceeded to add a few more. My Dad started walking back down the hill, heading toward his own garage, "he was walking fast, which was never a good sign," his legs were so long that his one-step equaled 5 of my own. Mr. Benny was following behind us, and he, too, had picked up more of the gravestones and was bringing them to our garage. Daddy did not say much, but he thanked Mr. Benny after they finished stacking about 9 or 10 of the gravestones behind the garage. Daddy waited until Mr. Benny had walked far enough that he wouldn't hear him talking, "Let me tell you something right now, daddy said, looking at me with that stern face that meant business, "I was a little scared, I thought I did something wrong, so I just nodded my head yes and kept looking into his eyes, daddy was still kneeling on the ground from stacking the gravestones, "you are never to tell your mother about this, do you understand me? "Yes, sir I said. He walked over to the brick grill he had been building on the other side of the house. It was still in the early stages of his build. He stood there with his arms crossed, studying his grill. I guess he may have been trying to figure out where he could use the stones. Daddy worked a little while longer before we went inside for the night. The next afternoon, daddy went to the back of his garage and pulled out an arm full of the gravestones. I guess he had thought about it enough and came up with an idea of how to use them. Daddy laid about 4 or 5 of the stones on the part where the charcoal would be placed prior to grilling, and he added one stone on each of the built-up sides to make it look fancy.

    I got where I did not like to get close to the grill. It was well made and big, and it matched our house perfectly. Daddy had made it from the left-over bricks from our house built, and the patio it was built on was from some left-over concrete from the build also. Daddy even bought a picnic table and put it beside it, so we could have cookouts, but I did not want to eat out there, I would get chills just being close to it, and I had an extremely uncomfortable feeling like I was at somebody else's house, and they wanted me to leave. My daddy only used the grill once or twice, which was odd because most people would have loved to have had a grill and picnic area like that.

4

Paranormal

The hovering airplane was not my first experience with paranormal things. In 1968, my great maternal grandmother Tula had passed away in the house that she and my grandmother Kelly shared. She was a very spiritual woman of God, an active member at the Holiness Church that she had attended for many years. She was strong in her faith, and she lived straight by the bible.

She was a tough disciplinary person, who gave a new meaning to *"Spare the rod and spoil the child."* If she had a house full of grandkids over, and one of them did something bad, and she didn't know which one it was, she would line everyone up at the kitchen door, where you had just one opportunity to confess. If not, she would ask us one by one to point out who did it, *"in which most of the time we would just shrug our shoulders with our hands up in the air, like I don't know? Cause we weren't about to be *the rat."* Still, that answer would ultimately mean she spanked all of us. Her philosophy was if she got all of us, she knew she had got the one.

    Great-grandma Tula was the matriarch of that side of the family, and when she died, all the children and grandchildren took it hard. Immediately after my mother heard of her passing, she got us kids up, and she and my dad drove to my aunt and uncle's house. My uncle Scott was my great-grandmother's last-born child. My mom put us in the bed with two of my older cousins Barbara and Alice, so we could go to sleep. My cousin, Alice's bedroom, had three doors in it, she also had her bed positioned with the headboard against a back wall, this position of the bed made the foot of the bed face all the doors and one of those doors opened into a dark, cold basement, that they use for parties and family gatherings. They kept that door locked at all times because it had a separate entrance from the backyard so people would not have to come through the house when they had parties. But most importantly, they locked it for safety reasons.

    Within a few hours of my great grandmother's passing and trying to go to sleep in the small crowded bed, I looked up and in the doorway between the basement door and the door to the hall, I watched as my deceased great grandmother walked through the closed basement door in the bedroom, then walk about 10 feet straight across to where the hall door was. *"It was already opened,"* she turned left, and that was as far as I could see, she never looked at us in the bed, and since the two doors were adjacent to each other in the bedroom, I was able to watch her as she walked across the floor from door to door at the end of the bed. She had a stoic look on her face. I sat up and started crying and pointing in total confusion, telling the older cousins what I had seen. They tried their best to calm me down. Still, I did not understand why they had not seen her. I wanted my Momma and to go home, but that was not going to happen that night because back in those days, many families would bring the bodies back home. Besides, my parents and uncle had already left to check on my grandmother since my great-grandmother had died in her arms just hours earlier. She was devastated, and rightly so. They also had to get grandma's house ready for when the funeral home would be bringing her body back for the viewing.

It was so creepy to see my great-grandmother laying in a coffin in the same room where she drew her last breath. This was the first death that I was aware of since I was just a small child. With all the cousins and other relatives crying out of grief, it was hard to understand what was happening because most kids do not know what grief means. My mom did her absolute best trying to make us understand in the simplest way she could. She said, *"great-grand momma Tula went to be with Jesus in heaven yesterday."*

"But momma, I just saw her last night?" But my mom would just repeat the same thing about heaven and reassured me that it was because she was watching over us if I did see her. I was not sure I was buying that answer and starting to question why I was seeing this stuff and not everyone else?

Haunting of Barrington Heights Estates

 I spent the night with my grandmother Kelly, a short time after my great grandmother Tula had passed away. Grandmother's house had been built in 1930. And it was a big White Victorian two-story home with 8 bedrooms. It had dark hardwood flooring. With the combination of the poor lighting, it made for a dreary place resembling an old funeral home. It had heavy sliding doors in every room and one extremely tiny door in the hall that we could not touch. Grandmother did not have a bathroom downstairs at that time, so at night, we had to pee in an old coffee can, *"God, I hated that."*

 My grandmother's bedroom was at the back of the house, she had a lot of shelves that went up the back wall a few feet from the foot of the bed, and that is where she kept a bunch of dolls for the kids to play with. They were old, and some of them had movable eyes that were creepy at best. There were a couple that felt eerie when you played with them. One was the tall walking doll, you could hold her hand, and she would take steps. When it was time for bed, my grandmother would pick up all the dolls and put them back on the shelf except the tall doll, she was too big, so grandmother left her standing on the floor at the end of the bed.

 Bedtime was something I feared no matter where I was, that's when terror would set in, and the darkness of the night would make me feel like I was in danger. Grandmother did not use a nightlight, so as she would fall fast asleep, my heart would start beating faster and faster because I felt alone. The house became awaken in the darkness. It was a cold, damp feeling. Since there were no streetlights, the darkness made me feel like I was in a closed box, just waiting for something to happen. The darkness at her house had texture to it. It was like a thick cloud that you could move through the night if you put your hands in it. I would constantly see movement in the darkness. My heart raced, waiting for a face to come through the thick dark cloud. I could feel the dolls watching me from the shelves at the end of the bed. It was a horrible feeling. The room felt so crowded, as though they were standing all around the bed. All I could do was get my body in the tightest ball I could to protect myself and try to keep my eyes as wide open as I could without falling asleep.

How am I going to explain this to my mom? And would she even believe me? after a couple of times of this happening while spending the night with grandmother, I would not spend the night with her again and became leery of dolls.

The strange happenings had started to take a toll on my little spirit. And unfortunately, it was only the beginning
....

I was incredibly close to my paternal grandmother Ida. She was a fantastic cook and baker. She taught my mother how to cook when she married, as well as Kat and me, and I am proud to say we all turned out to be rather good cooks.

Grand momma Ida was a top-notch seamstress. Her skills were impeccable, she had made all her own clothes and our Easter dresses when we were little, and with the quality time I spent with her, I too learned to sew.

Haunting of Barrington Heights Estates

I was still quite young when my grandfather passed away, so I would spend the weekend with my grandmother from time to time through the years. Since I had a terrible experience at my other grandmother's house, I would still get anxious about the nighttime and being away from my parents. One weekend, I went to stay with her. Like most older folks, she went to bed as soon as it had gotten dark outside and got up at the crack of dawn, but not me, I would find anything and everything to talk to her about to keep her talking so she would not go to sleep. "Both she and my Great grandmother Bess had a dry sense of humor, and she would tell me funny stories about the two of them as she grew up, but eventually she would say, "ok that is enough talking for tonight," and off to sleep she would fall, and I would feel alone in the darkness again. However, there was one good thing though, my grandma's house was in the city, and it had a streetlight that would give a soft light in the room. Her house was so quiet and still, and when you are already afraid, your hearing instincts kick in even stronger. The sound of the Tick Tock, Tick Tock , and the chimes of every passing hour of my grandfather's wind-up clock continuing repeatedly echoed through the house," I thought my head was going to explode from the repetitious rhythms." I was so tired, but sleeping just was not going to happen. My grandmothers' mother, "my great grandmother, had not long passed away, and my grandmother had kept her mom's glasses on her dresser. My eyes were drawn to the dresser for some reason, and with the soft light from the streetlight, I could make out where a few items on the dresser, "Including the glasses, were placed. Suddenly two eyeballs popped up in the glasses. I started shaking my grandma to wake her up. I was in panic mode. She calmed me down and tried to convince me it was a dream, but I knew what had happened, and no, I was not dreaming. The only time I closed my eyes was to blink. I felt like something was wrong with me. I had not heard any other children talk about things like this.

It was not long after this incident that my daddy's brother passed away. He had an amazing sense of humor and was always picking with the children in the family. I was so sad when he died. It was only a few days after he passed that I went outside to play basketball in the backyard, "daddy had lowered the basketball goal so that I could make the goal." I started playing and had only shot at the goal a couple of times when I started positioning my feet and holding the ball over my head, concentrating hard on the net before I would take the shot, the same way that I always had, when my deceased uncle Tony appeared sitting on the top of the backboard! He was sitting in a rocking chair, "rocking back and forth, just as happy as he could be, on top of the backboard, that was only feet away from me. I froze, dropped the ball, and took off running straight for the house, hollering the entire way for my momma." Momma, Momma, Momma!!!!!! "Uncle Tony's sitting on the basketball goal !!!!" What, momma said? I repeated louder, "Uncle Tony is sitting on the basketball goal. And she just said the same thing she had said about my great grandmother Tula." Well, he is just watching over you, that is all.

Haunting of Barrington Heights Estates

These events were getting harder and harder for me to understand, but nothing could have prepared me for the next phase of this paranormal world.

A few months had passed since this happened with my uncle Tony, and my grandmother Ida came over to spend the day with the family. One of my friends, Amy, and her younger brother Steve, got their much older brother Randy to drive them over to my house. They had called and said they wanted to show us a baby squirrel that they found in their yard. I met them in the yard before we all went inside to show my mom the squirrel. Steve kept referring to the squirrel as he. My mom asked," how do you know it's a he? Steve, with his snaggled tooth grin, started turning the little squirrel around in his hand when a little red wiener came sticking out, and Steve answered, "that's how. All of us were laughing so hard, including Grandmother Ida. Momma had taken both her hands and covered her face as she laughed. Well, all righty then, she said with a big grin.

We talked a little while longer, and then we all headed outside. My mother and grandmother were talking while we got in a quick game of hide and seek. Amy and Steve turned around and started counting. Since I needed a quick place to hide, I decided to hide in the storage room under the carport. I closed the door as quietly as I could and faced the door, so I could hear them coming, "9 10 ready or not here I come they shouted." As I stood there in the darkness, I felt something come up behind me and stand close to my back. I became frozen with fear, and the chills covered my body from head to toe. I started hearing my own heartbeat in the darkness, Lub dub, Lub dub, Lub dub, but I still could not move, that is when I heard another heartbeat that had rhythms different from my own, ba-dum, ba-dum, ba-dum, and I knew I was not alone. I finely built up the courage to leave the storage room, but I came out a different little girl from the one that had gone in just minutes prior. The darkness in the house had officially introduced itself.

5

This House is Making Me Ill

It was the Fall of 1972, and the house was revving upon its already malevolent ways. It had grown tired of opening and closing the hall door and leaving the lights on. The spirit had begun to come into my room every night, and when it did, I would often run down the hall to my parent's bedroom. I would be crying while I explained to my mom that something was in my room. She would comfort me for a moment, then take me by the hand and take me back to my room. After a few times of begging her not to leave me in that room alone, I would tell her because there was something bad, like a ghost in there trying to hurt me. Her reply would be the same, "Ghost, can't hurt you!

I started realizing that I was on my own with this issue and rarely talked about it at home anymore. Even though

Haunting of Barrington Heights Estates

things were getting so bad, I would ask God to take me to heaven if I had to live like this. I started vomiting a lot and had severe stomach pains. My mother took me to the doctor, and they put me in the hospital to run some tests. The test revealed I had stomach ulcers and lymph nodes in my stomach. The doctors were puzzled about these diagnoses because I was only around 10. The doctors would always ask, "what are you worrying so much about?" I would just say, "I don't know." Because I knew they would not believe me, so it was just easier to keep it to myself and suffer in silence.

The lousy spirit had started a more aggressive attack on me that would go on for years. He, yes, "he, "would wait until everyone else was in bed asleep, "I was always the last one to go to bed." I would crawl in the bed, lay on my back or left side to watch the door as I had done for years. About an hour in, I would feel his energy in the hall starting to build up. It was the most intense feeling of dread and horror. I would feel cold in the room. The temperature in the room would drop about 15 degrees. I would feel him as he crawled on the end of the bed, then slowly moving as he would make his way up my body. As I would lay paralyzed on my back with both arms by my side, I could feel a heavy pressure on my chest, and he, with his monstrous long face and unhuman features of an exceptionally long nose and long chin, would hover over my face, looking me straight in the face," like a lion would right before he ate his prey." He did not touch my face, but you could not have got a hair between our faces. After what seemed like forever, he would crawl back out the room, leaving me in tears and despair, praying for God to protect me.

I never knew what the next night would bring, but it was always going to be something. I knew that for sure. The bad spirit was increasingly getting stronger. I felt like he was draining me of my blood like a vampire. As I got weaker and always at the doctor's office with something, "He" started shaking my full-size heavy mahogany bed! He would shake it so hard and vigorously that I thought he would throw me off the bed! If he can do this, what else was he capable of? I was trapped and held prisoner and had no control over my own life.

I moved my bed to a different side of the room to get a better view of the hall. With the foot of the bed facing the doorway, I started noticing hundreds of balls of light, in all different sizes in the hall and my doorway. Each one had a light inside, some were brighter than others, but they were all round and ranged in sizes from pea size to the size of a quarter. I did not get a necessarily bad feeling about it, I thought that my eyes saw molecules as we had studied in school, so I rationalized it as, "I must have some good vision if I can see molecules.

My Friend Amy came to spend the weekend with me, "she was a little scared at my house, but she had never had anything bother her. We were in bed talking, and she had to go to the bathroom. She was gone for a few seconds when she ran back into the room breathless and shaking and waving her arms in the air. "what's wrong? I said?" she said this dot just chased and attacked me down the hall! At that moment, I knew that what I had been seeing was not some special x-ray vision. I told her what I had seen in the doorway and confirmed that what she had seen was real, and I believed her. I was afraid she would never want to come over to my house after that encounter. I realized there were other spirits in the house after that. I had never heard of a spirit orb. There was not much information about things like that back then.

Even though I was not fond of dolls, I did have a time when I was interested in ventriloquist dolls, and I did receive two for Christmas one year. I had a large Charlie McCarthy and one named Danny O'day. I found that I was not particularly good at it, "No Jeff Dunham career here, "so I retired them in one of the two closets in my room. My closets had bi-folding doors, and the closet on the left side of the room had an uneasy feeling about it. To cut the light on in the closet, you had to pull a string attached to the fixtures chain. The spirits would taunt me at night by cutting the light on in my closet, and through the slats of the folding closet doors, I could see both Ventriloquist dolls staring at me from the shelf. I would have to lay there until I got the courage to get up and cut the light off.

In 1974, my friend Jenny came over for a sleepover. She had already had an encounter with the spirits from a previous visit. She had been sitting in the chair that was in front of the sliding glass door. Since the glass doors would let in so much heat, my parents had installed very heavy drapes, and as she sat there, this very heavy drape lifted off the floor and completely wrapped around her upper body, including her head. The only thing visible was her lower body from the kneecaps down. This left her very startled, but Jenny had an inquisitive mind, and even with my warning of the danger, she wanted to see more. Against my better judgment, we sat down outside by the old cemetery fence, with one of those board games that no one should ever play.

"Sorry for my own wellbeing. I refused to call it by name. If you are familiar with the paranormal, you already know the name."

As we sat there asking our questions, I felt sick to my stomach. I was so mad at myself for risking more attacks. I was not sure why I did it. Maybe it was the hope that the board would offer information about why this was happening to me or answer what they wanted. As we dusted off our clothes and headed inside, I knew that I had unleashed something else, and there would be significant consequences for my stupidity. We had gotten our baths and ready for bed, and we talked for a bit afterward. I could feel the most negative heavy energy come into the room, that's when loud funeral organ music started playing; it was so loud that I was holding my ears and screaming, this woke my mom, and she ran into my room, "what is going on in here she asked?" Don't you hear it, momma, I said?" Hear what, she said?" The funeral music was blaring from the wall. "No, I don't hear anything." I looked at Jenny, and she said, "I don't hear it either." I could not believe it; my head was pounding from the organ playing the same thing over and over, and the cords played were of a death march.

Haunting of Barrington Heights Estates

My mother started questioning us about what we had been up to prior to this happening, so I told her, and she said, "Where is that game? Give it to me now, and you are to never play with it again. She took it out of the room and put it in her office.

The music played most of the night. Since Jenny couldn't hear it, she finally went to sleep, leaving me alone in my torment. The morning was not much better either. We had awakened to the smell of what I would best describe as a "dead rotting rat. The odor was so pungent that I almost threw up. I started sniffing every inch of my room, trying to find out where the smell was coming from. It didn't take long before I had found the source. It was coming from the same wall where, just hours earlier, the funeral music had been blaring. The smell of a rotten carcass lasted for weeks before it finally dissipated as quickly as it came. It was not long after the smell had vanished that the board mysteriously popped back up in my room. Staring at it in pure disbelief, I went straight to my mother to ask her why she would have brought this game back into my room after all that had happened that night. "I didn't; she said," I think her seeing that the board game had made it back into my room had scared her. This thing has got to go!" she said, and right then and there, she had decided that she would have to drive it off somewhere and dump it far away from our home.

Before I graduated in 1980, I was in the hall bathroom brushing my teeth and getting ready to go off for a while. I had my head down toward the sink as I rinsed my mouth, and as I lifted my head to see myself in the oversized mirror, my reflection was that of an incredibly old wrinkly lady. She laughed or made a spooky grin. I fell back against the wall. I was just shocked. Every time that I was in that bathroom and needed to look in the mirror, I would work my eyes up slowly from the sink or wall to prepare myself for what might be staring back at me.

The haunting moves outside.

It was the summer of 1982. I was now 19. My parents had been saving to get my mom her big dream inground pool. The installers were outside digging this enormous hole. I felt weird vibes coming from the dig, so I stayed away from it until they finished digging it out. Right before they installed the lining, we decided to enter the pool to see just how deep it was, so we entered at the shallow end and walked down to where the belly of the muddy bottom was, and as I stood there looking up at how far underground, we were, I had a chill come over me from these negative feelings of doom that filled the empty cavity, and I knew this was not going to play out well.

A few weeks later, the pool was finished, and it was a hot afternoon. Nobody was home, so I decided to get into the pool. As I stood at the glass doors, I had a nagging feeling making me question my decision to go swimming alone. I was a fairly good swimmer and had never feared the water. I had learned to swim at an incredibly young age. I decided I was overthinking things and talked myself into going. I floated around for a while then swam to the deeper end of the pool close to my dad's garage. After swimming back and forth a few times under the diving board, I started dog paddling back to the shallow end. I positioned my body so that my legs and toes pointed downwards with the thoughts of just moving my arms back and forth until I felt the bottom. I was 5'11, so I knew I should be touching it soon. Suddenly, I felt as though something had grabbed my legs and was pulling me under the water; and as I popped my head back up out of the water gasping for air, I would be submerged again, no matter how hard I tried, I could not move my arms or legs, it was as if I was paralyzed from the neck down, but even though my mind was in a full panic, I knew that I would drown if I didn't get to the side of the pool. After bobbing up and down for what seems like forever of a slow, painful drowning, I started to get a slight feeling back in my arms. I managed to twist my exhausted body to the side of the pool. I knew something wasn't just out to hurt me but was now trying to take my life.

6

Nobody is Leaving This House

It was Fall 1982, and I was getting ready to get married. I was excited to get out of that haunted house. I was still battling bouts of illnesses and was hopeful my health would improve after I left. However, I was worried about my family's safety as well. They still weren't convinced that there were ghosts in the house. I knew that if the spirits did not have me to feed on as their full-time energy source anymore, they would be looking for other ways to feed in order to manifest themselves. It takes a tremendous amount of energy for spirits to do what they were capable of doing in that house. And I knew the spirits were not going to leave just because I had.

A few weeks before my wedding, I had a doctor's appointment to get a physical, since I had been battling all kinds of infections for years. I had a very noticeable enlarged lymph node in the side of my neck and under my arms that had been there since I was 17. I had been to see the doctor so many times about it, only to be told it was nothing and was most likely coming from my low immune system and recent infections, so he did not think it was cancer. My GYN said," have you had that lump in your neck checked? Yes, I have, I said multiple times. "Well, I want you to go see a surgeon right away."

"What?" I was shocked. Do you think something is wrong, I asked? I am worried about that for you, and you must get it removed. I left her office shaking and alone. I sat in my car to wrap my mind around what I had just heard. Does she really think I had cancer? I am too young to have cancer. I have not even turned 20 yet. I am still technically a teenager.

My GYN had scheduled my appointment with a surgeon within that week, and my mom drove me over to his office. After the examination, the surgeon did recommend a biopsy asap. I told him I was getting married in less than 3 weeks and asked him about scarring and the recovering period since it was a large nodule that would require many stitches that would go from one side of my neck all the way around to the front. I had never had surgery before, and I was just overwhelmed with everything on my plate.

After the surgery and the biopsy was sent off, we began the waiting game, and one evening my mother got the call that they had a preliminary report with an "undetermined diagnosis." We kind of felt a little comfort for a minute and had hopes that it would be nothing, and I put my focus on my wedding day.

The wedding day was finally here, and I was extremely nervous. I wanted it to be perfect; after all, it was my dream wedding, the kind that lives in every little girl's mind as a child. The church was filled with red roses everywhere, and with the delicious food, the huge multi-layer wedding cake with its dripping red roses and waterfall, that was almost too high to cut, we shared our day with 250 family and friends. It really was a fairytale.

I was sick during our honeymoon, I guess the adrenaline of the past weeks had stopped working, and I was glad to be going home to our house. On the way home on the last day of our honeymoon, I stopped by my friend Amy's house to pick up something she had for me, her phone rang, and it was my mother. Why are you calling me over here, mom? "Well, I need you to stop by here before you go home." "What's the matter? Did you hear something from my results?" I asked. "Yes, everything is ok, but I need you to stop by so I can tell you about the report." "You cannot tell me over the phone," I said. "We had been traveling. I wanted to go home." "No," she said. "I need to explain what he said, ok? See you in a minute." She hung up quickly, so I could not ask her any more questions.

When we arrived at my parents' house, they met us at the door. My mother never cries, so when I saw her at the door crying, I knew, and I said, "I have cancer, don't I?" "Yes," she said, both of my parents were just as devastated as I was. We all cried together as a family, and I asked, "what kind of cancer I had," and she said, "Hodgkin's Disease Lymphoma, and your cancer is in stage 3." Well, I knew there were only 4 stages of cancer, and 3 was not good.

Since I had found out while on the last day of my honeymoon, I felt this was an omen. As the months passed, I had lost 50 pounds from the treatments, and I was already thin before I started them. My parents asked my husband to get the marriage annulled because I needed their care full-time, and besides that, were both so young to have to deal with something like this, and we had only turned 20 years old less than 3 months prior, and this would be a long-drawn-out thing, but my husband said no. But ultimately, my parents were right, and I needed them to take care of me. I could barely walk. I was 5'11 and 95lbs, and a shell of the person I used to be. I was just a thin layer of flesh hanging over a Skelton, it was a horrific sight, and my daddy didn't even want me to walk around because he was afraid that the bones in my legs would snap into. If you have seen a very anorexic person in the end stages of that disease, that is what it looked like.

It was too much for a young couple, and we did end our marriage. But what I realized is I left the house on the day of my wedding to start a new life away from the hauntings; only to find out on the last day of my honeymoon, five short days later, I had stage 3 cancer and was back living and sleeping in the same damn bed in my old bedroom just weeks of leaving. (Think about that a minute) The spirits would just not let me leave alive.

As soon as I was able to get on my feet, I got a full-time job. Even though my hair had not all come back, I was just so excited to start a new life, and since the home that my dad had built my mother as their first starter home, "the place that I lived my first five years of life," was still owned by my parents, I moved back there. It was not until a few years later that a negative spirit started to let his presents be known. It made it difficult living there. It seemed like no matter where I was, the spirit world would find me.

At almost eight years later, to the day of my biopsy, my sister Kat," 28 years old at that time, was getting a nodule removed from the same spot on her neck that I had mine removed. It was shocking when we heard the heartbreaking news that she, too, had been diagnosed with the identical cancer stage 3, Hodgkin's Disease Lymphoma. The doctors had let it go way too long because they believed it was impossible that siblings would have had the same kind of Hodgkin's Disease that we had. We ended up being the only two sisters with identical Hodgkin's Disease in medical history. They did find a brother and sister case later. My sister battled hard, and she did recover.

It was 2002, and I had remarried and looked forward to a new life when my life changed again. We had been married just over eight months, and almost 20 years to the day that I got diagnosed with cancer in 1982, and Kat's diagnosis eight years after that, a large fist-sized lump popped up in my breast, I knew as I looked in the mirror at my reflection, that here we go again, and the next few days proved me right. I was diagnosed with stage 3 breast cancer. It was aggressive, and the oncologist that had treated me for my first cancer did not give much hope for survival, so I changed doctors. I started seeing my sister's oncologist, and she did not give me all the gloom and doom. She said it was going to be extremely hard, but you can do it! Because of how aggressive my cancer was, I had to take strong chemotherapy. I had to sign an agreement that the treatment I would be given WOULD cause damage to my heart. I signed because I would not have lived long without the treatments, and true to the agreement, within months of treatments, my heart was in unbelievably bad shape, and I was diagnosed with Cardiomyopathy. I returned to my full-time job even though my doctor was against it, but I had to try.

In 2007 My Daddy, one of the greatest heroes in my life, was diagnosed with stomach and throat cancer. He passed away before the end of that year. We were so devastated. Our family is extremely close and had been through so much together. It was such a void in all our lives. Shortly after my dad's passing, I was picking up my mother at her house, I remembered looking at her as she walked down her driveway, and I thought," she has cancer. I could feel it on her. My mother had always been extremely healthy, and she ate well and worked out. A few weeks later, we found out that she had Non-Hodgkin's Lymphoma Disease stage 3. Unfreaking believable! She finished her treatment and was finally in remission. Just about a year later, she would be diagnosed with Parkinson's Disease, of which there is no cure.

A couple of years had passed, and she had started having pain in her abdomen, and her doctor ordered some tests. The test revealed a diagnosis of Ovarian cancer stage 3. After surgery and another round of chemotherapy for over six months, she went into remission for a short time before it reappeared again in 2016. This would mean more chemotherapy all over again.

We did not know it then, but 2016 would be one of those years that was unbelievable, the kind you start saying to yourself, "no way, no way, this shit cannot be real." But unfortunately, it was very real. I was 53 and in full-blown heart failure with only six months to live. My mom's cancer had come back, and my sister Kat had gotten diagnosed with stage 4 Sarcoma-cancer, all this within months of each other. My sister and I lived about 5 miles from one another, and we did not see each other much because we were both so sick. The closest we got to each other would be as our cars would pass going in different directions, on the interstate in another state 300 miles from our homes while we both were seeking treatments from some of the top specialists in the country. The drive was long and hard and was 4 to 6 hours one way if there was traffic.

Getting a heart transplant was my best option of survival, but with a history of the spirits and my special abilities with the paranormal, I was not about to take the chance of taking a heart from a person that had just passed away from an accident, or other non-related instances not related to the heart, and their spirits not being able to accept their own passing.

Haunting of Barrington Heights Estates

I learned as I got older that I was clairvoyant. Some people call it a psychic medium since I can talk to the dead and see things that others cannot. Often people would say, "what a wonderful gift to have. "No, I would say, I would not wish this on anyone! It has been a blessing at times, but also a curse! With my luck, I would get a person that had been on death row and in solitary confinement for the last 30+ years at a maximum-security prison! Let's just say that heart might just come with a little attitude problem.

Try to explain that reason to your doctor why you do not want to get this precious gift of life. I am incredibly supportive of people who are organ donors, but no way would I chance this. Just a little FYI, if you tell your doctor this, then look at your watch, and see how long it takes to have a psychologist show up in your hospital room, yep, you will be getting this visit. I quit sharing things about my feelings and why I would not have a heart transplant. I was lucky enough to get an LVAD in the summer that year. It is a mechanical heart that is life support and patients live completely battery operated.

Within months of getting open-heart surgery and having so many complications, things were so bad that my home health nurse asked to be reassigned to a different patient in fear that I would pass away during her visit. Still, in the battle of her life with her treatments, my mother had come to my house to check on me. She, too, was very weak, and as she watched the tears run down my face from the pain, all she could do was kiss me on the top of my head and tell me she loved me. There was nothing she could do but watch as her child was clinging to life. As she walked out the door, we both knew that there was a chance that we might not see each other again. And just like her visit with me, her visit with Kat was not any different, things were dire, and the chance of losing 2 of her three children, "I just cannot imagine: being a mother myself. My sister Dawn took care of our mother while my husband was working full-time and taking care of me, and Kat's husband took care of her, as all 3 of us continued to hold on to life by a string.

Less than three months later, my sister Kat lost her battle with cancer, leaving behind two adult children, her husband, and a loving family. Kat was only 56 years old. I was still in critical condition and unable to attend the funeral. It was a very deep dark time, full of depression and loss, just a feeling of complete helplessness.

7

Memories of The Zombie Man

It's late 2018, and the last couple of years have proven to be especially hard on our family. Losing a family member leaves holes in the souls of the ones who remain behind. With my mother and I still dealing with debilitating illnesses, all we could do was to live our life day by day, moment by moment.

It was a cool December morning; I got a call from my mom:

"Hey, how are you? she said,"

"Good, how are you feeling?" I responded.

"I am hanging in there." she replied.

"Listen, something is going on with my trash can."
(Trash pickup service comes every Thursday)

"What is wrong with your trash can?" I asked.

"I think someone has put a curse on me!"

"Wait a minute momma, repeat what you just said?" I asked.

"I think someone has put a curse on me."

"What kind of curse?" I kind of giggled to myself.

"I do not know, but I feel like someone is trying to scare me, because I am an older woman, and all along on this dead-end road."

"Ummm, you do not believe in curses momma!"

"Well, all I can tell you is I think someone has put one on me, I can feel it. Someone has tied a plastic bag full of cotton to the lid of the trash can, and I cannot get the darn thing open."

I was thinking how strange it was for my momma to talk about anything like curses.

In fact, it had been a while since we had talked about anything paranormal. I think the experience we had in Connecticut in Feb 2014, had really started changing her mind about the spirit world. She and I went to Foxwoods Resort and Casinos for a few days for some much-needed therapy(lol).

Haunting of Barrington Heights Estates

This was the second time we had ended up in a blizzard during a Connecticut trip. Foxwoods is one of our favorite places to visit. It is on an Indian reservation, just like almost all casinos. But this one is incredibly special; it is beautifully decorated in a Native American theme.

This is where I go to buy my sage for my house cleansings. For whenever I feel a negative energy around, and since I will only buy sage on an actual Indian reservation, this is always a must stop at the resort for me. I enjoy the positive energy of this beautiful quaint shop full of unique Indian treasures.

Since Foxwoods is one of the finest resorts in the country, with more gaming than Las Vegas, it is truly a hidden gem that most people have never heard of. It is situated in the middle of NOWHERE, USA.

We would always schedule our trips when we felt better, it gave us something to look forward to, and we always had a great time together. During this trip, we stayed at Pequot, 'Foxwoods has about 3 or 4 different hotels under one roof. All the hotels are beautiful with large rooms, but Pequot rooms seem a little bigger.

After we got our keys/card, we went up to our rooms to wait for the valet to bring our luggage. It had gotten dark outside and as I opened the door, I saw a multicolored ring on the window, about the size of a fist. I stood there staring at it and asked mom if it looked familiar to her. She answered, "Yes, yes, it sure does."

It was the same ring that we had seen while on an airplane a few years prior and that had followed us for hours before disappearing. I thought to myself, "*I do not know how I feel about seeing it for the second time, because there are always meanings behind paranormal sightings.*"

We went and got something to eat before we headed to our favorite slot machines where we spent a couple of hours. It was then time to get back to our room for the night. The next day was pretty much of the same, eat, gamble, shop, eat, gamble, eat, and then to bed, repeat. On the third day, I received a message from the Rhode Island (PVD) airport telling me that our flights for the next morning had been canceled due to the blizzard, and that the airport would be closed for the day of our departure.

"Oh well" momma reacted.

So, we went to the check-in and paid for another night, and I booked a new flight.

Since the roads were icy and we had to return the rental car too, I did not want us to be rushed after checkout, because it was a long drive to the airport. Still not knowing for sure if that one would also be canceled, but for that one extra night, it wasn't a big deal. Besides, they had an ATM machine(lol).

Our favorite game was *roulette*, and we were good at it. This is one of those rare occasions I enjoy having some psychic capabilities, it is not 100 percent, but it is fun to challenge the strength of my abilities, especially with colors and numbers.

The casino had been quiet during our visit because we were snowed in, so we did not have to wait to long for a table to play. I had seen a table in the middle of the casino floor that had only one person sitting on the stool. *So, I said, "come on momma, let us sit here and play for a while."*

I didn't pay much attention to the man, even though I was sitting right beside him. Although in my peripheral vision, I noticed him as an older gentleman in a beige-colored suit, but I was busy getting out my money.

"Roulette was serious business to momma and me." *LOL*. It wasn't but a few minutes into playing that I noticed a coldness in the air around my left shoulder, all the way to my feet. We were sitting side by side, but not touching. It was a feeling of walking into a commercial freezer, which came from the man sitting on my left side. I don't recall hearing him speak a word; he would just nod at the dealer and place his chips at the beginning of the games. I slowly turned my head to get a better look at him because I didn't understand why I was getting such a chill from the quiet older man. My mouth dropped, and I yanked my head back around straight. I was facing the table once again, and I could not believe what I had just seen. I was shaken to the core.

The man next to me wasn't alive, he was a zombie or some kind of time traveler! He was solid like any human being. He was wearing an antique wristwatch. Since I am familiar with different types of fabrics, I recognized that his suit was made of linen, but not of our times. It was not woven as tight as today's linens are. Moreover, it had more texture to it, nonetheless, it was undoubtedly an expensive suit.

His skin was gray, *"the color of gray clay that only comes with death.* He had no heartbeat, no moving veins, he was dead! The chills were unbearable, and his energy wasn't a good one. I looked over at my mom, and with my eyes wide opened to the startled mode. I asked momma to cash out and leave the place. Momma turned her head to the side and squinted her eyes as if to say, *"What is wrong with you?"* I gave her back a big eye stare again, *"We need to go back to the room."*

We collected our chips and went to the cashier to exchange our chips for cash. While walking she said, *"What happened back there?"* I said "Momma, that man sitting beside me was dead. *"What? He was dead!"* Momma didn't question me about it. I was on high alert walking back to the room for our last night. I felt a negative energy all around me that I couldn't shake.

When we got to our room, our key didn't work. I said, "SHIT!" I wanted to get into the room and lock the door, because I felt like someone was watching or following us. So, we headed to the front desk to get another key, and then went back up to the room. The feeling had intensified, although we had never felt unsafe at the resort before.

Walking into the room had a disturbing feeling to it, and not the same feeling it had when we had arrived days earlier. It was now cold and creepy, honestly, If our luggage hadn't been placed there (close to the door), I would have thought we were in a different room. Finding my laptop on; and its glaring light filling the darkroom, I felt a chill that went all the way to the bone.

As I walked towards the laptop to take a closer look, I was startled. It was still plugged in the same outlet that it had been plugged in for days. Still sitting on the ottoman right where I had left it. However, I didn't leave it on… and room service had not even cleaned our room yet because they were shorthanded due to the blizzard. I squatted down in front of my laptop and watched as the batteries died right in front of me, despite it charging all day. I knew in that moment; we were not alone in the room.

Spirits will steal energy from anything that produces it, like humans, electricity, batteries, or anything that has power, and with thousands of bright flashing slot machines with bells constantly ringing, plugged in all over the resort, makes for the ideal place to have a haunting or solid full-body apparition.

I looked up at momma and said, "He followed us."

"Who followed us, she asked?"

"The zombie man from the roulette table."

"Well, he better leave." she said jokingly.

She went to take a bath, and I started getting us packed so we could leave the next morning. As I stood there packing, I noticed that the ring had faded significantly on the window. Momma finished her bath, and I went in to get mine. Since momma had already fallen asleep, I left the light on in the bathroom. I closed the door, just enough to create a soft light in case we had to go to the bathroom during the night, before I crawled into bed. I watched TV for a while in order to calm myself from the uneasiness I felt in the room and took my Ambien to help me sleep.

When I got sleepy, I turned the TV as well as my overhead light off, leaving only a little bit of light coming from the partially closed door of the bathroom. I faded off to sleep. Around 1:30 a.m., we were awakened by a sound that was so loud that we both sat up in our beds at the same time. As I sat up, I realized all the overhead lights were on over my bed.

"What the hell!" I exclaimed. It was so loud in the room that momma jumped up, running towards the window to pull the drapes back to see if we were in a tornado, or some type of bad storm. The noise in the room sounded as if we were standing alongside a long, never-ending train that went roaring by. The kind of sound to compel you to put your hands over your ears to spare your eardrums. Clickety-clack, Clickety-clack, Clickety-clack over and over again non-stop.

When momma pulled the drapes back expecting to see a massive storm, what she found was far more disturbing,

"Complete and utter calm." Not even a snowflake was falling. *"What's going on around here?"* She uttered.

In her nightgown only, she quickly walked over to the door of our room, unlocked it as fast as she could, slung the door wide open, expecting to find something, she found NOTHING. She stuck her head out the door, looking in both directions, for anything or anyone. Not satisfied with finding anything there, she became frustrated and even more determined to solve the mystery of where the blaring train-like noise came from. As she held on to the doorknob with one hand to keep it open, she walked out the door as far as she could without letting the door close behind her. She stood there in the empty hotel hallway with only her nightgown on. It was completely quiet, just the dead silence of an empty hotel.

It was quite possible, that we were the only ones on that entire floor because we were still snowed in. As momma turned around and walked back into the room, she realized that the sound wasn't in the hallway. As soon as you crossed through the door frame of our room, you could witness something unworldly.

As the horrific truth stared us both in the face, *the sound was coming from inside our room!* The deafening noise was just an explosion of pure force and power, that continued to swirl around the room like a vortex of train cars. The experience really did a number on my mom's nerves; she had never experienced anything like this before. There was not a way to explain it or to deny what had happened during that long night. As the dawn shined its light on the resort, the sound dissipated. We dressed quickly and decided that we would get the hell out of that room anyway that morning, even if our flights were canceled again. And we did.

8

The Curse

The Zombie Man experience always stayed in the back of my mom's mind, even though some years had passed. Mom had not had anything else happen like that before, and I think when the trash can lid had been tied down, she started having these strange feelings around her, and the only thing she could compare it to, was the last night we had spent at the Foxwoods Resort, and how the haunting of the *Zombie Man* made her feel helpless and tormented by something she could not see.

In the last days of that December 2018, one of the neighbors had spotted my mom while she was out and about running her errands. They asked her if she knew that a portion of the Stephens family's property had recently been sold.

"No, I had not heard that, did they sell all of it or just the portion of the property where they had the stables?
"You know that is a commercial property due to the access to the main rode, and that their property backs up to ours?

"Yes, I knew that." said the neighbor. "I bet who ever bought the Stephens property would love to get their hands on yours too.

"I am sure they would, momma replied."

The next Wednesday night, momma took her trash cans out to the road between her front yard and Mr. Benny's Garden, just like she had been doing for years. The next morning my phone started ringing around 11 am.

"Hello, well, it happened again, momma said."

"What! you are kidding me, I responded!"

"No, I am afraid not, she said, they did the same thing again, they tied it so tight, it took two of us to get it untied."

Ok, I thought, Humm, this is getting a little strange, because there were no kids in the neighborhood anymore, and most of the neighbors were older folks like momma who were original to the neighborhood, and as for those who had passed away, their children had moved back into their childhood homes. Moreover, everyone knew each other there.

Still, just like 1965, when my parents originally purchased the property, there was only one way in, and one way out. Since the road was so narrow, and if two cars happened to be on the road at the same time, one would have to go off to the side a bit. Even the trash service truck would back down the hill due to the limited space to turn around on the narrow road.

After thinking about it all day, I called my mom back.

"Mom," I said, "I am not sure what is going on, but I think I am going to get a security camera installed before next week's garbage collection. Maybe it is the newspaper carrier since they deliver around 3:30 a.m. every morning, thinking it is a funny prank or just doing it for pure meanness,"

By the weekend, we had installed a camera under the carport, and one on the column on the front porch, and turned them toward the road where I had a view from the top of the hill, all the way to the dead end. Wednesday evening, momma pulled the cans to the road, and around 12 a.m., I started watching from the security app that I had downloaded during the installation of the cameras. I was able to see well in the darkness with the help of the camera's night vision.

"At 3:30 a.m., I watched as the newspaper carrier slowly came down the hill and put the newspaper in the paper box, then back down the driveway. I thought, "HA, I got you now! I waited patiently for him/her to exit the car and walk over to the trash can, but he/she just sat there with his/her foot on the brakes and never got out of the car. It was not long before the car left the driveway and headed back up the hill. I stayed up about an hour more going through all the video, to see if I had missed anything from the time my mom had pulled the trash cans to the road, but other than the newspaper carrier, no one else had come down the hill.

My phone rang that morning before I had gotten up,

"Hello," I said.

"Hello, well, check your camera," she said.

"What?" I responded.

"It happened again," she said.

I said, "no way Momma!"

I watched almost all night. I told her, there was nothing going on except for the newspaper drop off. Let me call you back momma. I spent the rest of the morning watching over and over and going back and forth between the camera's footage. I had a huge area of coverage all the way past the dead end and the Stephens property. Apart from that, Mr. Benny and many other neighbors' homes were visible in the video. I was able to see the back of the trash cans and did not see anything hanging or unusual on the backsides.

So how did the bags get there? I had a visual on everything, even the road. I would have seen anything big or small walking over to the trash cans and tying a bag to the front side. Even if they were crawling on their bellies, I would have seen them. I spent hours in the next day's going through every detail of that night's live video recording, using all the camera's zoom capabilities. I looked in the wooded areas to see if, by chance, any homeless person had snuck into the woods to set up a camp or something. I even went back to the days prior, looking for anything out of the ordinary, such as people walking at night.

There was nothing, absolutely nothing. There wasn't a human being around except for the paper carrier, and they didn't even get close to the trash cans. I knew it wasn't anything human that had tied that bag to that trash can, *period.!*

I had a sinking feeling coming over me. *Maybe momma was right* about the curse, because it stopped after the 3rd time, and paranormal spirits often incorporate the number 3 in their malevolent deeds.

It was a few weeks into the New Year of 2019, and my mom called me one morning, *just as she does every morning.*

"Good morning!" she said.

"Good morning to you, and just how are you feeling today." I asked.

"I didn't sleep well last night." she replied.

"Why not?" I asked, *"I had two little girls scratching on the screens of my bedroom windows!"*

"What? Hold on a minute momma," ok I said, "tell me that again one more time!"

"She said, I had two little girls scratching on my bedroom windows screens."

"Momma, how do you know it was two little girls?"

"Because I heard them talking and giggling outside at my windows." she said.

"Which windows momma?"

"All of them." she said.

"Even the one behind your bed?"

"Yes." she replied.

"Momma, that window is too high up for a child to reach!"

"I don't know, but that's what happened." she said.

"Well, maybe you were dreaming that you heard children outside."

"No!!! I was not dreaming! It was around 1:30 a.m., and they woke me up."

"Well, why didn't you call us?"

"Well, I just didn't. I just went and peed and crawled back in the bed and went back to sleep."

"Ok momma, well let me check through the cameras to see who these kids belong to, ok?"

"Ok, I will talk with you later then, Love you, bye."

"Ok momma, love you too."

What the Hell is going on here!!! I pulled up last night's video and scanned through all the way until daylight, and there wasn't anybody outside during the night or the earlier hours of the morning. However, I did see momma's bathroom light come on shortly after 1:30 a.m., just like she had stated in our earlier conversation. I backed the camera's video up to look at what was going on in the hours prior to her getting up and going to the bathroom, and I listened carefully. I didn't hear or see anything, except for the occasional frog and cricket serenading the night.

My mom had never been afraid to live there alone, even after my dad had passed. She had always felt safe there. It had been her home for over 50 years. The only thing that had frightened her, was the trash can incident, but that had stopped. Besides that, we had cameras that would alarm my phone if a person or car even came close to her house.

Since my mom did have Parkinson's disease, and one of the symptoms was possible hallucinations, I had to include that possibility in my thought process. Even if that was the case, that doesn't explain the trash can incident. We had no indications that she was hallucinating. I talked with her all the time. So, I told my sister Dawn, that I wasn't sure what was going on, but I didn't believe she was

Haunting of Barrington Heights Estates

hallucinating. With all the hell I went through in that house, I had to keep the likelihood of it being paranormal in the back of my mind. The house had never picked on momma or haunted her before, but I was on high alert now, and could feel the energy in the house shifting to something negative.

9

Sunroom Visitor and A Doppelganger

A couple of weeks had passed without any incident, until I got the dreaded call from my mom telling me what she had found that morning.

"Hello, good morning." she said, *"Ummm, someone has gotten into my sunroom!"*

"What?" I said.

"Someone has been in my sunroom!"

"How do you know that momma?" I asked.

"Because they have been sitting in my chaise lounge."

"How do you know that momma?"

"Because, they have taken my towel that I keep folded at the foot of the lounger and moved it to the middle of the chaise lounge and left it there all wadded up."

"And not only that," she continued, "but I can see where someone has been sitting."

My mom was an immaculate housekeeper, and that towel had always been folded neatly at the bottom of the chaise. I sat there in silence for a minute to gather my thoughts.

"Do you think that you left the glass door opened last night?"

"No! It was locked and I checked it again this morning after noticing my towel had been moved and it was locked."

"Ok momma, ummm, I don't know what else to do, except to order another camera to put in the sunroom. I will call you later momma, bye. "

I wanted to go look through the videos from both cameras to see if anyone had come down the hill. Besides, my phone hadn't notified me of any unusual activity last night.

My search came up empty.

Mommas' sunroom was a lovely area off the kitchen and eating area. It had large glass windows and doors that overlooked the sparkling blue-looking water of the pool.

The tall multi-tier water fountains musical droplets dancing on the water, made for the perfect ambiance in her private oasis. Momma would often spend her day reading or napping out there. So, I had to figure out what the hell was going on.

I ordered another camera and was hoping to have it installed by the end of the week. Momma's house would have more security than Fort Knox. A couple of days went by, and I called her when I got up:

"Good morning, how are you this morning?"

"I am Ok." she replied.

"Guess what?"

"I am afraid to ask, but what momma?"

"My visitor was back in my sunroom last night."

"Wow, this is starting to get ridiculous."

"Well as soon as the camera comes in, we will get it installed, ok?"

"Ok then, bye."

Before we could get the camera up, her visitor had come back again for the 3rd time. When the camera order finally came in, my sister Dawn met us at Momma's to help us install it.

Haunting of Barrington Heights Estates

Since the camera had great range, we put it facing the doors that went out to the pool, as well as the side door. Being in this position, I could see all the items in the sunroom, especially the chaise lounge. This way, I would have a clear visual of anybody who was in the sunroom or backyard. Even though the backyard was double fenced in *because of the pool,* I had a good view of everything I needed to see, and all alarms were set for notifications to my phone.

It was time for Momma to go to bed, and just like every night, I made her call me when she was in bed and ready to go to sleep. I had all 3 cameras going and I was ready! Around 12:00 a.m., I had an alarm go off on my phone to check the sunroom area. It had picked up some motion and noise.

I could watch all the areas at once but depended on the alarms in my phone to pinpoint any movement or sound I may not have seen or heard, and these cameras were extremely sensitive, and I trusted them 100%.

I clicked on the alarm, and it took me to the video of the sunroom then I clicked on the highlighted picture, and I put my ear to the phone, expecting to struggle to hear a faint little noise of some kind. **BANG***!* I yanked the phone from my ear, then cuffed my hand around my entire ear because it was ringing so badly from the sudden burst of the unexpected noise. "**WTF**!!!!" I thought, *"someone has broken it to the sunroom and busted all the glass out!"* My Heart was about to jump out of my chest! I cut the volume off as much as I could on my phone and watched the video expecting to see glass everywhere on the floor of the sunroom.

There was another set of sliding doors behind the sunroom's camera, that opened up into the kitchens eating area, but those were locked every night, and the doors also had a special stick in place for extra security. It would have taken the fire department to come In, and bust out those heavy doors. So, whatever it was, or whoever it was, that had made that explosive noise, I knew that they were not in the main part of the house with Momma.

Then I heard another **BANG!** *I had learnt my lesson about holding my phone that close to my ear.*

The best description of what the 'Bang sounded like, would be if *a person were to throw a heavy rock the size of a brick off a bridge, and it went through a vehicles window.*

I looked the entire video over to see what was broken and where the noise could possibly be coming from, but again, nothing, no broken glass, nobody in sight.

I sent the video to Dawn the next morning to get her thoughts.

"What the HELL was that from, she asked?"

"That's what I am trying to figure out."

We both were dumbfounded and genuinely concerned for what would be coming next.

Almost every single night around 12:00 a.m., for the next few weeks, the same thing happened repeatedly, . Some nights it would happen again around the 3:00 hour. It was like someone was toying with us.

I got a call from my mom one morning, and I could tell she was talking with a little 'nervous excitement when she spoke.

"Something happened right before dawn this morning." she said.

"Oh God, What?"

"There was a man standing at my bedroom door, but I couldn't make him out completely, and I could hear another man calling out, 'Brian get up, get up!' That voice sounded like it was coming from the sunroom area."

"Well momma, you know that house has always been haunted, even if you don't want to believe that."

"Well, I am not leaving, so we are going to have to get along. she said.

It was a Saturday Spring morning, and my mom calls:

"Did you need something last night?"

"What?" I said.

"Did you need something last night?"

"No, why would I? I talked to you when you had gotten in the bed last night momma."

"Well, you walked into my room and stood at the edge of my bed and was staring at me, then you looked over at the phone sitting on the bedside table."

"What?"

"Yes, it was you, and I thought, well if you needed something you would've called. So, I rolled over and went back to sleep."

Momma knew it was a spirit, she thought it was my spirit checking on her. But unfortunately, I think it was a doppelganger, or a poltergeist disguised to look like me in order to make my mom feel safe. They wanted mom to take her guard down.

The nightly bangs and sounds of breaking glass had picked back up and had escalated. This went on constantly at night without any visual explanation.

10

Hispanic Ghost Party

It was about mid-month of June 2019, and keeping true to our nightly routine, momma calls me when she gets in bed to go to sleep. I had no idea when I went to bed that night, that the next morning would be the beginning of many horrendous events that would change our lives forever. This next morning, I got the most disturbing phone call from my frantic mom.

"Hello," I said.

"I had a horrible night last night!"

"Why, what happened?" I asked.

"The tv in the den woke me up blaring,"

"What?"

"The TV in the Den was on and blaring."

(Momma's den was large. My dad had closed in the original 2 car carport and storage building in the early 90's. After the renovation of the new den was complete, Dad added on an additional extra-large 2 car carport to the new renovation, with direct access to the new den area. *"Basically, another house."* Since our family was growing, we really needed that extra space, as family time was especially important to all of us, and this was the perfect solution, plus momma would get her big fireplace that she had always wanted, and with the space from the old den area, my parents put in a table in there that would accommodate almost everyone for Sunday dinners).

I knew momma hadn't left the TV on, because she cuts everything off before she goes down the hall, and she would have noticed the noise as she headed off for bed.

"OMG momma, did you go cut it off?"

Momma replied, "I got up out of bed and walked slowly to the end of the hall." She further explained, "when I noticed a room full of Hispanic people laughing and talking loudly, and some just kept on watching TV. I walked slowly up to the opening of the den, and they all started looking at me! I started yelling at them to get out of my house!!! What are you doing here !! Get out! I turned around and walked towards the hall, and they were gone."

I knew we were in trouble at this point, and we talked about getting the house blessed, but I also told her that sometimes a blessing can be risky. It can anger the spirits even more, making things worse.

It was the weekend of that same week, and I got an alarm on my phone from the sunroom's camera late morning. I could hear clearly Hispanic Music playing. So, I called my mom over the security camera's microphone.

"Momma?"

I heard her say yes from the other room.

"Are you watching a Mexican movie?"

She said, "NOPE!" "You hear that, don't you?" she inquired.

"OMG, yes! where is it coming from?"

"I don't know," she said.

I was freaking out! What were the chances of Mexican music playing all around the entire house the same week that my mother had an awful experience with a room full of Hispanic spirits?

I frantically pulled up every camera around the house, and could clearly pick up the Spanish music, coming from all 3 cameras! The music level didn't shift from camera to camera for me to zone in on a particular area where it would be the loudest. It was the same tone level on every camera, so as I listened to the male singer belt out his song accompanied with a violin, and other instruments playing in the background.

I realized that the music sounded like it was coming up through the ground. I listened off and on all through the afternoon and evening hours.

At exactly 11:00 p.m., the music just stopped, and what is even more chilling, is that the Mexican singer had been singing, which sounded like the same song, over and over again for about 12 hours!

"This is some bullshit right here." I said to my husband!

Since I knew firsthand the capabilities of a malevolent spirit when it came to music. The sound of that funeral music playing repeatedly that night that Jenny had spent with me so many years ago, still haunts me to this day.

The next day my mom called up to Mike's house. *Mike had purchased Mr. Benny's house after both Mr. and Mrs. Benny had passed away.* And like most of the properties in the neighborhood, after an owner had passed away, a relative would move back to the home, but Mike wasn't kin to the Benny's, but he was kin to the Parks family that had lived next door to the Benny's since 1965. And Mike was aware of the old Cemetery in his backyard as well.

"Mike, did you happen to hear any Spanish music playing yesterday?"

"Yes ma'am," I did. It had gotten on my nerves after a while, so I called the police to file a report about "whoever it was," disobeying county noise ordinance, but there was only one problem though." Mike said.

"Oh really, what might that be?" Momma asked.

"The police could never pin down the exact location where the music was coming from."

Momma called me after she had spoken with Mike to fill me in on their conversation.

I said, "Well, momma, I think we know where it was coming from!"

"It's coming from the cemetery in Mr. Benny's/Mike's backyard, and your property!"

Momma's health had started getting worse. She had truly little energy anymore. I knew that the spirits were really starting to feed on her energy since they were getting strong enough to manifest.

We were still in the month of June, and Momma had stopped by my house after she had finished her doctor's appointment. We sat on the couch and talked for a while about everything happening.

Then we walked outside, and talked a little more while standing by my car. Momma got quiet for a second, then she told me that a male spirit had come into her room while she was sleeping and grabbed her by the arm!

"What!"

"Yes!"

"I was sleeping on my left side, and he grabbed my right upper arm, as if to get me to roll over, and I turned my head toward him with a mean look on my face, "like what are you doing?"

"OMG Momma, demonstrate on my arm exactly what the man did to you." I told her.

Momma turned to me and grabbed my upper arm.

"OMG!" I said, "Momma when spirits start touching you, that means things have gotten out of control, and will only escalate from this point. I am very worried about you being there by yourself."

"I am not going to let them run me out of my home," she said. *"I just keep praying for God to keep me safe."*

11

Busy Spirits

I had always let my sister, mom, and husband know that I would never ever spend the night in that house again! *I would tell them; Bill Gates doesn't even have enough money to make me spend one night there*!

I hated even being there for one minute by myself! The malevolent spirit known as, *"He"* would start bothering me the very second I was alone. And God! I hated to walk down that hall day or night. I guess it really wouldn't fall in the category of walking down the hall, it was more like a sprint!

Once I started speed walking through, I could feel all these spirits just trying to grab at me, especially between my old bedroom and the formal living room. Well, it wasn't the formal living room anymore. We had turned it into a formal dining room some years back. It had been beautifully decorated, and Momma was able to display some of her special older pictures of family, past and present, on a side round table, that she had custom-made, just for that purpose; and it looked great in front of the window.

However, you never felt alone in that room. The same feeling was true when it was the formal living room, nobody wanted to be in there. So, the White furniture always looked brand new. That room had a feeling like it didn't belong with the rest of the house; like it was an afterthought addition, but it wasn't. It was part of the original build.

After I would pass those 2 rooms, I still had to speed walk past the hall bathroom; and once I got past that room, I would head to mom's master bathroom. Things were calmer in there.

I would often just sit in my car and wait for someone to come before I would enter that house. But even if I was perfectly healthy, I wasn't spending the night in that house., Oh HELL NAW!!!! That SHIT would never happen.

… The last time I had spent the night up there, was 2 days after my dad had passed. My sisters and I wanted to stay close to our mother during this difficult time. I was petrified and I begged my old friend *Amy* to spend the night with me up there. She agreed to, but I told her I was not sleeping in any of those bedrooms. I brought 2 blow-up mattresses for us to put in the den between the lazy boy recliner and the desk and put it as close against the fireplace as I could. She said, "That's fine."

I was scared all night and dozed off right before dawn. That's when I felt my opened sleeping bag, which *I used as my blanket, started to move downward, towards the floor. I pulled it back up under my neck and started to doze off again. A few minutes later, I felt a pulling at the bottom of the sleeping bag, and I felt my opened sleeping bag as it moved at a steady pace down to my knees. I sat up and woke up Amy to tell her what just happened. God, I hate being at this house!*

There wasn't a safe place in this whole Damn House I thought!

Every room had bad memories, it seemed. Even the bathroom in the Den had a checkered past. It had been renovated from the storage room. The one that I was playing Hide and Seek in when I was little, and the bad spirit had come up behind me, and I heard another heartbeat other than my own.

What I did know is you can make any room something else, but its walls will always remember what it originally was, no matter the decor or space you make it into. When a house is built, it is born, it is created from an idea, and an idea is energy, because it is made from the most powerful thing in the world – the mind.

In early July, Momma had gone out to check on the pool pump. It looked like the water wasn't circulating. The pump had quit running, so she opened the power box, and that's when she discovered that all the wires had been mangled and twisted. Momma called Ray, he and his wife had a lovely home on the lot that we used to play baseball on when we were little kids. He had a vacation home that they spent a lot of time at. So, I was glad he was home that day.

Ray was an excellent mechanic, so momma called him to see if he could just look at it before she called an electrician. Ray said, "Sure Mildred" and he came right over. He was shocked at what he had seen.

"Mildred, you mean to tell me that this was like this when you opened the box?"

"Yes, momma confirmed.," well this is unfixable, Ray replied."

I called him to ask about it since I didn't see the box. I wanted him to explain it in a way that I could understand.

He said, "Raylee Anne, I have never seen anything like that in my life, it is humanly impossible for someone to do what I have just seen."

I could tell that seeing this had really shaken him up as well.

Momma had to call an electrician to get a new one, and I started going over the video footage again and again. And just like before, There Was Nothing!

Momma said, "I told you I have a curse on me. Whatever this thing is, it's trying to make me move! It wants my house or property. But I'm not moving, and I keep telling it that!"

12

Voodoo Ladies

It was later in the month of July; Momma was awakened again by the same spirit (he *was the one that stood in her doorway when she heard another spirit in the sunroom who was asking Brian to get up. I don't think this is the malevolent spirit,* he wasn't trying to hurt Momma like the other one that grabbed her arm.

He walked over to the bed and told her that Holly was causing all these bad things to happen to her. He also told her he wouldn't bother her anymore, and that he wouldn't be back for 100 years.

Momma was so upset while telling me everything that had happened that night.

"I have never done anything to hurt anybody. So, why would someone want to put a curse on me? Besides that, I *only know one person named Holly, and that was Holly Stephen's, and we were friends"* Momma said.

Holly Stephens and her family lived in the unusual Bi-level house with the 3 different accessible roads. This is the commercial property that had sold in the last part of 2018. it backed up to Momma's property.

Holly had died about 20 years ago, and her husband had died years prior to that. The neighbors had been told of her death right after she had passed. A relative of the Stephens family was at one of the neighborhood cookouts. When momma asked about the time of the funeral, their relative told her that there wasn't going to be one, and that the family had decided to have a private memorial.

About a week after the visit happened with the spirit telling Momma about Holly, I started getting alarms from both the cameras around 9:40 a.m., on a Saturday morning. My alarm notification stated that the cameras had picked up someone talking. I went to the live video so I could see who it was. It was 2 African American ladies getting out of a vehicle. Not too many people came all the way to the dead-end fearing as there wasn't a way to turn around.

At first, I thought, Ummm, maybe they are from a local church or something and just wanted to leave a pamphlet, or to invite people to their church. I wish that had been the case.

As I zoomed my camera in, to get a better look at these 2 ladies, a dreadful feeling came over me. Both ladies were dressed in bright yellow outfits, like an Easter outfit. The problem was it was an outfit from the 60's or 70's. My first thought was they look like some of the ladies that practiced voodoo in New Orleans.

One lady was plus size, and the other one was thin. Both had strange hats. Nothing felt right about this scenario. As they walked down the sidewalk, I zoomed in to the plus-size lady's hand, because she looked like she had a twisted fingernail that was painted in a leopard's pattern that went almost to the ground. When the ladies made it to the front door, they rang the doorbell. Thank God my mom didn't answer.

I zoomed in on the thin lady, she was acting spacey and her hair under her hat looked very strange, with a style, from what I could see under her hat, of the 60's. They stood there for the longest time before they started walking back to their vehicle. Once they got in their car, they just sat there in the driveway for the longest time. I was thinking, what the hell were they doing? I zoomed in so I could look at them sitting in the car.

They looked stressed or agitated. Their entire facial expressions had changed, just creepy as hell. They finally left and headed up the road. I went back to the video to take another look at every detail because this had greatly disturbed me. I studied every step they had taken and zoomed in at the maximum capabilities that the camera would allow. My eyes were stuck on the plus-size lady's fingernail again.

"Who in the hell has one 30-inch fingernail for one thing. If you did, would you paint it a leopard print, while wearing a 1960's Easter dress?"

I observed that fingernail closely, and then I gasped, "*OMG, that was a snake.*" I sent my sister all the videos and the snaps, she was totally freaked out. I called my mom and told her to never open the front or the carport doors, *even if someone came and rang the doorbell.* I asked her to wait until I could identify them through the cameras. I also advised her to close all her blinds that faced the front of the house. I reminded her that my camera would notify me if anybody came down the hill, so I would be able to see them before they got to the door. We also let everyone in the family know to call before they came, or they wouldn't be let in!

The following Friday after the 2 mystery ladies had shown up, my alarm sent me a message stating it had spotted someone on the front cameras. So, I clicked on the alarm and started watching the live video. I saw a pickup truck, and it turned around in the driveway before it pulled up to the mailbox. I watched as a woman got out of the truck from the passenger side and put something into the mailbox. Then she got back in the truck, and they drove off. I wasn't too alarmed, and thought she was just putting a flyer in the box trying to sell something. That afternoon my mom called me,

"Hello."

"Hey, you are not going to believe this one," she said.

"I am afraid to ask Momma, but what?"

"I just pulled out a flyer from my mailbox that had a Missing person on the front."

"What?"

"And guess who the missing person is?"

"Who momma?"

"Holly Stephens," she stated.

"What!"

"Your Neighbor Holly Stephens that's been dead for 20 years?" I spoke.

"Yes, it is, and there is a picture on the front of the flyer of her."

"Wait, wait, wait!" I said, "give me a minute Momma, to wrap my head around what you just told me. You mean to tell me that just a couple weeks ago a spirit tells you that Holly was making these things happen to you, and then you get a flyer with 'Holly's picture on the front of a flyer, a woman that we had not seen in 20 years, even though she was technically your next-door neighbor?"

"Well, I don't know what's going on here," Momma said, but there is a telephone number on the flyer asking for information."

"Ok, momma give me that phone number and I will call it. This must be a scam."

I called and left a voice mail with my phone number.

I had a bad feeling about that flyer. I don't believe in coincidences, and as crazy as all this shit was, I knew it was somehow connected to one another. I didn't get a return call, but it kept me up all night thinking about it.

The next morning when I talked to Momma, I told her that I was going to send Drew (my husband) up there to pick up the flyer, even though I had a bad feeling about bringing that flyer in my house. I needed to read what was on it.

Momma said, "Well, I have already thrown it away."

"Well, can you get it out of the trash?"

"I don't know, I will call you back if I find it."

About 30 minutes later she had found it. I sent Drew up there to pick it up. I was anxiously waiting. As soon as it was put in my hands and I looked at that picture, I could feel bad energy coming from it. It was a picture of Holly Stephens on the front. I noticed she looked much older than she should have looked for her age, since she had died 20 years ago.

It was puzzling. I sat down and went through the flyer carefully; a copy of Mrs. Stephens's death certificate was in there. It showed she had died in 2013! No, this is impossible, Mrs. Stephens had died around 20 years ago, so that would have been around 1999. No way, this is right. After all, the entire neighborhood had thought she had been dead for 20 years. So, where has she been if she has been missing all these years?

I called the number the next day

This time I said, "Well, you need to call me, because I know where Holly Stephens is." I left my number again,

I thought, well, this ought to get a response. It wasn't long after I placed that call when my husband came from outside and he said, "Mr. Gray Cat is dying."

What?

Mr. Gray Cat was feral; he would visit us daily and seemed to enjoy laying in the sun from our back deck. He had done this every day for about 8 years; he was a loving and perfectly healthy kitty.

I jumped up and went to the back door, and there on my deck laid our beautiful Mr. Gray Cat. He was suffering as he gasped for those last few breaths of life. Someone had poisoned him and killed him. We were devastated. He had appeared on that same back deck when he was only about 2 months old. We were heartbroken. Did this flyer have something to do with this? I wondered. The feeling of dread was coming from that flyer. I looked at my husband and told him to take it down the road and get rid of it instantly! He said he would do better than that. He said, "I am going to burn it!"

He buried Mr. Gray Cat in our backyard right beside the deck he enjoyed so much, and where we had first laid eyes on him so many years before. The place that our eyes would meet one last time. We wanted him to be close to his favorite spot. My husband burned the flyer. But we both knew that it was somehow connected to all these bad happenings coming from Momma's house.

13

They Know Everything We Say

Things just kept getting worse and worse. Momma had started sleeping a lot more in the daytime, and it was more than just a nap. I told momma, "Just come and stay with us for a while. But she said no that she was staying at her house and sleeping in her own bed!

August wasn't much different. Momma would be awakened often by the sounds of people walking up and down the halls at all times of the night. The sunroom camera was still sending me alarms almost every night in the form of *Bangs* and *Crashing* noises. She had also heard the children scratching again at the windows. But again, there was nothing to see on the cameras.

I did, however, pick up something strange later that month from the front porch camera. My alarm had sent an alert that it had picked up a person talking. So, I started listening to see who it was. I could clearly hear 2 men having a detailed conversation about an air conditioner, and I was able to zoom in and locate where the voices were coming from this time.

"It was coming from the middle of the cemetery, and there was not a human in sight! The interesting thing about this was I had called my mom the day before to get the phone number to the company she uses for her air conditioner repairs. So, I could have someone come and look at the unit at the other property she owned. At the very same time, that I was listening to the 2 men's conversation over at the cemetery in the backyard of Mr. Benny's/Mike's property, my husband was calling me to inform that the air conditioner repairman had arrived. *My husband was doing repairs on the property, and just happened to be there when the repairman arrived, because the repairman wasn't sure when he would get there.*"

My husband told me that the 2 of them were looking at the broken air conditioner, and crunching some numbers to see how much it was going to cost to put a new unit in.

This was almost the same conversation I was listening to live from the front porch camera, *but the repairman and my husband were at a house 10 miles away from mom's!*

I was startled, and I knew that these spirits were listening and watching everything we were doing. So, mom and I had to start talking in code words when we were on the phone to keep them from knowing what we were talking about.

In the following month of September, Momma had been awakened from her sleep when the overhead light in her bedroom came on in the middle of the night. As she sat up in her bed to see what was going on, she started hearing the clicking sound of the light switches, as one after another was being turned on until all the lights were on in the entire house, including the outside floodlights!

She got up and walked down the hall, and as she stood there, she started hearing the clicking sounds again, as one by one of the light switches, *"starting from the den at the front of the house and working its way back to her bedroom; cut off each light, and she found herself standing alone in the darkness with only a night light that softly lit the hallway.* She was startled and had no choice but to just go back to bed.

My sister Dawn and I talked with our mother, begging her to get out of that house!

"Momma," I said, *"if you don't leave, this house is going to kill you! Look at yourself right now, you are so sick and weak. You can hardly get around." I said firmly!*

"NO!" she said, *"I am not giving up my home!"*

"Well, you will die soon then momma; because that is what they do, they want to suck every bit of life from you, and not only that momma, but you must also understand,

that this house could be torn down to the ground, and another one built in its place, and the same thing will happen repeatedly until the end of time. It's the Land momma!"

My sister Dawn owned a lovely home across the street from where I lived. She was in the middle of updating it, trying to decide if she wanted to sell it or not. She had offered momma to come move into her house, until we could figure out what to do further.

I also advised momma that if she didn't want to move into Dawn's home, maybe we could find her a home in our neighborhood that she could just buy. This way, she could make it her own and have a fresh new start. *At this point, we just wanted our mother close to us, so we would be steps away from her, instead of miles.*

Momma said, "Well, we will have to see."

I guess that was better than her firm NO!

Momma still had hopes that things would calm down and the spirits or curse would soon tire and just go away.

We had entered the Fall 2019, and Drew and I stopped by to drop off my mom some supper. When we entered the den, I felt uncomfortable, as if 100 eyes were watching us from all different angles. The room felt very crowded, and I could feel eyes on me. My mother was a little sharp in her tone when talking to us, something that was so out of character for her. We kept our conversation very general because we knew the spirits *were listening to every word spoken.*

I said, "Well Momma, go eat your supper before it gets cold, and call me when you get into the bed."

"Ok," she said.

I was getting up from the recliner at the same time momma was getting up off the couch, as our eyes met to say goodbye. I noticed that mommas' beautiful blue eyes, had turned dark as coal. I had a knot in my stomach as she reached to hug me goodbye. And as we embraced, I turned my head away from her to avoid looking at her face, and I walked away without looking back. When Drew and I got back in the car, I was truly distraught over what I had witnessed.

So I asked Drew, "Did you see mommas' eyes?

"Yes, I did. They were Black."

I added, "Yes, they were."

He agreed.

"This is bad, what are we going to do?"

"What can we do?" Drew said.

"She refuses to leave; and besides that, who can we tell? Can you hear us explaining this to her doctor? What would we say? Well, listen doctor, my mom has some ghost

in her house, and she doesn't want to leave, but we really think she should. We think they are trying to kill her!"

"Raylee Anne, you know we will come out looking crazy right? Nobody will believe us!

"Yes, I know," I said. "And momma had asked me not to tell anyone, she doesn't want anybody to know, in fear they will think she is losing her mind from the Parkinson Disease." In desperation, I told momma to pull out every bible that she had in the house and go from room to room and tell the spirits that "In the name of Jesus Christ they must leave! And she agreed, and said it was worth a try.

Momma went from room to room, placing a bible and saying a blessing in each one. She was exhausted and growing weary.

14

Just Let Them Have It!

Around the first week in October, Momma was awakened again by the TV blaring in the den. Frustrated, she jumped up and headed down the hall. And once again, there was a large group of Hispanics having what looked to be a party in the den. Momma started yelling at them, "GET OUT! And a woman that was sitting on the loveseat and had her back to momma, turned around and threw both her hands up over her head, and said, **"I told them you weren't going to be happy about this!"**

Momma continued to demand they leave her house*!* But they kept on with their party; they didn't care what she said. Vanquished, she turned and went back to bed.

Momma, feeling defeated, didn't know what else she could do. She had prayed and prayed, for these things to go away, but they didn't. Even though we all knew momma's property was very valuable, especially with all the businesses continuing to be built all around her, and more to come since the Stephens property had sold at the end of 2018. It wouldn't be long before her property would be a goldmine. Dawn and I encouraged Momma just to leave it. Walk away, it had long been paid for. Just sell it, or don't; we didn't care about the money it may be worth down the road, just get out before they kill you.

It was the morning of October 19, 2019. Momma had just finished her breakfast and had taken a few steps into the hall. She was stopped in her tracks between my old bedroom and the formal dining room; when she felt someone come up behind her, lean into her ear, and whispered in her right ear: PLAN. YOUR. FUNERAL! In a male's voice.

My sister Dawn had called shortly after the incident, and my shaken mom was telling her what had happened.

"Let them have the house, Momma," Dawn said, "just let them have it!"

When I talked to Momma that morning, she was still on edge.

I said, "Momma, the spirit told you that basically, you are dead. He was telling you that he was going to kill you, plain and simple! Momma, all you have to do is say the word when you have had enough, and you will come live with us." I told her. "I know this is a big decision, why don't you think about it for the rest of the day. "

I told her that I felt that they were listening to our conversation, so we went back in code mode, because I was afraid it would try to kill her if it knew she was thinking of leaving!

I said we can come get you tonight if you decide to do *something* (code for leave). Or we can do 30 (meaning 30 minutes) I was shocked when she said 30! I said "Ok, ummm, without acting like somethings wrong, calmly go grab everything that you can get together, and we are on the way!"

My mother was coming out the door as we pulled up. She was running for her life. Drew jumped out the car and got her. Watching my 81-year-old mother walk away from everything she owned, with just a duffel bag full of clothes, her medications, and the clothes on her back, was heartbreaking!

She was so sick and weak and could hardly walk. So, Drew helped her into the back seat of the car. We left all her vehicles under the carport, and Drew threw the car in reverse as we sped out of the driveway, leaving her beautiful home in the rear-view mirror. I have no doubt, that if my mom had not left that day, that she would have died within a month.

Momma had left all her jewelry and cash behind. All she could do was to flee. Drew had to go back up there the next day because she had forgotten one of her medications. He ran in, then out quickly. He said he could feel a heaviness in the house.

Haunting of Barrington Heights Estates

October 22, 2019, I got a phone call from a person that was in part responsible for putting the flyer in the mailbox about Holly Stephens. I had almost given up on ever hearing from anyone from the event. I told the person that Holly Stephens had been dead for 20 years, I said, "so what's all this about! The person said, no, according to the death certificate they had obtained, she hadn't passed away until 2013, I responded with, "well, where was she all those years that we had thought she was dead? The person responded that she had been living in her house all that time. What? Yes, the person on the other end of the line said, I can't believe y'all thought she was dead for 20 years! I said, a relative of Holly had told the neighborhood many years ago about her death.

This explains something, though, the person on the phone said, "What is that I said. I was over for a visit with Holly around 2011, and Mr. Parks, who owns the adjoining property next to Mrs. Stephens, and Mr. Benny/Mike's, on the far side of the subdivision,

("both Mr. Parks and Mrs. Stephens properties, bordered the cemetery of Mr. Benny's/Mike's properties).

Mr. Parks was outside working in his garden, and as Holly and I were walking at the backside of her property picking Blue Berries one afternoon. Mr. Parks had lifted his head from working in his garden; and he yelped and jumped backwards,

"Holly? Is that you," Mr. Parks asked.

"Who else would I be," Holly replied.

"I thought you were dead," he said.

"Well, obviously I'm not," she responded jokingly.

The person on the phone expressed how that encounter had confused them both. And they wondered why people were thinking Holly had died.

Since Mr. Parks' wife was extremely ill, and he was her caretaker, he didn't get out much, so he had not shared his findings on Holly Stephens's surprise reappearance. Just as we were, along with the rest of the neighbors, still in the dark about that encounter.

The person told me that Holly had been quite ill for years prior to her missing or questionable death. And she, too, had been experiencing nightmares and unexplained paranormal activities as well. They also had found dead animals placed close to the house, with some evidence of a cult, possibly witchcraft-like activity in a portion of the wooded area.

"OMG," I exclaimed.

I told the person about my mom's encounters as well, and about the 2 African American ladies that had come to Momma's front door. The person stopped me mid-sentence;

"Oh my," they said, "Holly had nightmares about 2 African American women that she thought were into voodoo too. She was haunted by those dreams. "

I told the person on the phone that Momma thinks her property also had a curse on it, and the person said it probably does!

Not expecting that answer, I screamed out, "What?"

"Yes, but I can't tell you everything right now, but y'all need to be extremely careful right now;" they said, "in fact, I am worried about everybody in the neighborhood right now. And your mom is right, they do want her property."

Shaken I said "Well, Momma has moved out of her house."

I told the person I was very confused about why they had stated that Holly Stephen was missing, since they had a copy of her death certificate included in the flyer?

Their reply was, "Because where is the body? and we haven't any proof of her death other than this certificate, but things on the death certificate are inaccurate, so, yes, she is a missing person, and we suspect there may have been foul play. We have many unanswered questions that are not adding up to the stories we were told, and we need answers. We were very close to Holly, that's why we have been working so hard for years to find out what happened to her. And once the property was sold in 2018, a lot more questions began to surface, that are not corresponding to a particular timeline, with answers from a source that were very evasive. Please know that Holly loved your Momma and would never hurt her."

I said, "Yes, we knew she wouldn't, but it does play a role in all of this."

The person said, "We will be in touch later when they could provide more details."

And we said our goodbyes.

That call totally left me dumbfounded. Even the next day, I asked my Momma if that call really happened or was I dreaming? Momma said it was real, and she had heard every word of it too, and she was struggling also to wrap her mind around everything that was said.

Since Momma had only brought a few changes of clothes with her, she asked Drew if he was alright with going back into the house to pick her up some more clothes.

"Ok, mom, I will go back in there and pick up some for you," Drew replied, "just write down the things you need, so I can get everything at one time," he continued.

"Ok, thank you," mom said.

"Momma, we must be incredibly careful of bringing anything out of the house here. Spirits will be attached to things," I spoke.

"Yeah, you are right, I didn't think about that," said Momma.

I think momma really was hoping they would just disappear, but since Dawn had her things stored away, for her to paint and possibly sell the house. We decided that we would move Momma over there for at least 6 months until Momma decided what she wanted to do going forward, with a possibility of just buying Dawn's house. Since Dawn was painting and doing repairs to the house, Momma just stayed put with us. She started feeling so much better too. In fear of taking anything from her house that may interfere with her healing process, we started ordering her a whole new wardrobe. Drew would only go up there every other day to grab the mail from the mailbox and not go inside.

It was a couple of weeks into November 2019, I had a doctor's appointment. I asked momma if she wanted to go with us or stay at our house until we got back.

She said, "I really need to go back to my house and get some of my important papers together and things from my safe."

"Momma, I don't know if that is a good idea, you are doing so good, and I would hate to mess that up by you going up there," I said.

"Well, I think I will be ok, you won't be gone too long right?" she asked.

"No, we shouldn't be," I said.

As we came closer to Momma's house, I had an ache in the pit of my stomach, and as we pulled into the driveway I was just overcome with dread.

"Momma, are you sure you will be ok?" I asked.

She said, "Yeah."

So, Drew walked with her into the house to make sure everything was ok, and he also did a walk-through, then she closed and locked the doors behind him. We were gone less than an hour, and the woman that we left at the house, "who *was able to walk and talk*, was not the same woman that we picked up less than an hour later. Drew went inside to let her know we were back and found her in unbelievably bad shape sitting in her recliner. She said that as soon as we left, she had started feeling drained and had to sit in her recliner, unable to do anything. She was in such bad shape, that Drew had to hold her up completely to get her in the car. I thought my mother was going to die in the car on the way back to our house, I really did. And she didn't want to go to the hospital. I was so scared; I had never seen her look so bad in my life.

Momma was 100% positive that the spirits were trying to kill her, even after all she already had been through, this really terrified her. Mommas' health remained at a very fragile point. That one, 1-hour encounter set her back to a point, that she could barely walk.

Dawn had finished painting and Momma had all new everything ordered, new beds, sofa, etc... right down to wash cloths and towels, that was how afraid we were to bring anything from that house into her new resident. Everything was fine for a few days, very calm, and we thought, we were good. I was in Momma's bedroom helping my mom make her bed, when I heard a man talking in the hall, I stopped and called out, "Drew, is that you?" I didn't get a response, so I walked out the bedroom door into the hall, nobody was there, I thought, "OMG, I clearly heard a man talking in the hall. I thought, no way, no way this is happening, we didn't bring anything into Momma's new home.

Since I was going to stay with Momma until she felt comfortable in her new surroundings, I stayed on high alert, while Dawn was out of town.

After mom was in bed, I went into the kitchen and sat at the table, I watched as a black shadow came around the corner and then turned to go down the hall. I was paralyzed with fear for about 15 minutes, "I knew nobody was in the house, but Momma and myself. After I gathered my courage, I went down the hall, and peeped in on Momma, she was sound asleep, and no one was in the house. I was devastated, and finely went to lay down for a sleepless night full of unusual noises. The next morning, my husband came in and he said, "Well, let me take the cable box I brought from mom's house back to Time Warner Cable. (We had canceled Momma's service at her house, since she wasn't there anymore.) He said the box is on the barstool. "What! Get that out of the house! Why did you bring that thing inside," I said? "Well, I just didn't even think about that." Once he removed the Cable box, everything stopped.

15

Time to Investigate

After talking to my sister Dawn and Mom, I suggested that we call in a paranormal investigator, and they agreed. I reached out to South Carolina Paranormal Research and Investigations, they worked all over the state of South Carolina. With their impressive record of professionalism, I felt good about working with them. I explained what was going on at my mother's house and the severity of the situation. They were wonderful to work with and their team was able to set up an urgent investigation for November 23, 2019.

I warned him of the possible danger of these spirits, and that it wasn't a *"Casper the friendly ghost"* kind of spirit occupying that house. I also told him I was 100% sure they would get something. He assured me that they would take all necessary precautions before beginning the investigation for their personal safety. I also requested a house cleansing, to which he agreed. I additionally informed him that I would draw out the floor plans of the house and would mark all the hotspots.

The head team leader arrived around 6:00 P.M that evening, and Drew met him there to open the doors and to give him the signed contract. Drew also handed him the drawing of the interior and exterior hotspots in which included the first bedroom, (my old bedroom) and the formal dining room, momma's bedroom, the den, the desk in the den, hall bathroom, and sunroom. Outside, the cemetery, and my dad's big garage.

We allowed them free range of the house inside and out. The team leader called me a little after 11:00 P.M to tell us they were wrapping things up for the evening. I know y'all had to get something, I asked? Yes, we did; *I was surprised he said.* He also went on to tell me that 2 team members started getting bad feelings about coming to the investigation earlier in the day, and almost canceled, and that a couple of people had started feeling sick and had to go outside for a moment before continuing the investigation.

"*I wasn't really surprised by this.*"

He also, informed me that they had salted and did a cleansing as well.

"*We will have to go through all the video and audio to see just what we have from everyone's recorders, it will take a couple of weeks to go through all of it, but I will send you a final report along with a copy of any video and audio findings we have when we are finished with the investigation."* he said.

"Ok," I replied, "thanks."

Drew double-checked all the doors before he left. He said he could feel an unsettled feeling in the house. He could tell the spirits were not happy. Drew rarely remembers his dreams, but a few days later, he told me and my mom, that the night of the investigation, the spirits had taunted him all night long in his dreams, trying to convince him that he must kill himself. Drew was shocked that spirits had the ability to get in your mind, your dreams, your thoughts; but it was something I knew all too well.

While we were waiting to hear from the investigation, my nephew wanted to see if my mom would let him borrow her SUV. He needed to put his truck in the shop for a couple of days.

"Of course." Momma told him, *"You can come by and get the keys, but you will have to go to the house to get it"* ,she said.

"Ok mee-maw , thank you, I will bring it back in a couple of days." he said.

"Just take your time," she replied.

My niece was driving my nephew up there to drop him off, and as they got to the top of the dark hill, they both got the chills as she pulled into the driveway, still, he hesitantly got out of her vehicle to walk toward the carport. He said he was scared and could feel someone watching him in the darkness. He yelled back to my niece for her NOT to drive off and leave him.

My nephew was a former Quarter Back, a big guy, almost 30 years old, if this tells anything about the fear level these things are capable of creating in anyone.

As he was unlocking the SUV's door, he said he could almost make out a man standing right beside him. He was totally blown away because he had never felt anything there before. He left very shaken from the event.

We told my nephew to just bring the vehicle back to Momma's new resident, instead of taking it back over to the house. A couple of days later, he dropped it back off. It had a bad energy on it. I even thought I had seen someone sitting in the back seat. So, I got my sage out and we did a full cleaning on the outside and inside before anyone would drive it again.

On Wednesday, December 18, 2019, we received the final report of the investigation with video and audio. We knew the spirits were there from the many orbs that I had seen when I was growing up but didn't realize how many would come through during the investigation. I think they caught 9 different voices, including children. And we are sure they captured at least one malevolent spirit on 2 different recorders from their investigation of the formal dining room, and around the area of the round custom-made table on which Momma displayed some old and new family photos. There were 2 team members in there, and each of them was recording on different devices, and you could clearly hear a male spirit on (Audio Recording#9) say, "of course I have," on one member's recorder, and on the other member's recorder after the spirit said, "of course I have," you can hear the K2 meter go off.

(The K2 EMF meter is used by Paranormal Investigators by looking for sudden erratic readings (spikes) of the lights on the K2 meter. A man-made Electromagnetic Field (EMF) creates a steady reading while the spirit world's energy is believed to be what creates the impulse readings on the K2 EMF meter.)

They also sent a few videos. Two of them chilled me to the core; It was a video of their 360 Periscope.

(The 360 Parascope (Triboelectric Field Meter) was introduced in the Paranormal field as an aid for investigations; it follows static electricity fields horizontally, allowing you to be informed of the direction the field is traveling.

The team had put the 360 Periscope in the first bedroom (my old bedroom) and placed it on a table in front of the left set of closet doors. "Just where I had marked as a HOT-SPOT." The first video (Video#2) was from the camera placed in the hallway; there, we watched as team leader Shaun B. stated he had heard the Parascope activate, so he started walking towards the bedroom. At the same time, the Parascopes lighted static electricity (Video#1) was moving away from him. As if something was walking away as he walked towards the room.

Haunting of Barrington Heights Estates

The easiest analogy for me to explain what is seen on the videos, *is as if the spirit or energy that was in the bedroom was peeking around the corner to see what the team members were doing in the kitchen, and when the device activated, alerting the team, "that there were some activities going on in the bedroom. In other words, the spirit got caught peeking and started moving back into the bedroom.* I also noticed a few orbs floating around in the bedroom and in the hall area videos.

Seeing the bathroom mirror captured in the hall videos made me hold my breath with anticipation that the camera may have captured that old lady's face again in the mirror. Both these videos were frightening to watch, especially as the time displayed on both videos were in perfect sync with the event.

The next videos (Video#3 and Video#4) are just as terrifying. Watching as the Parascope sensor lights moved around as if someone was walking in the very same spot where I was tormented year after year by malevolent spirits, truly brought me great sadness. I felt sadness for the little girl whom no one believed. Sadness for the teenager whose health was stolen away, and sadness for the adult woman who still deals with the repercussions of living in that haunted house.

Hearing the little girl (Audio Recording#1) saying, "there is something on the shelf that can see us." It just blew my mind, especially after my mom was adamant about the little girls scratching at her windows. I read in the report that they had used an IR and GoPro camera that was directed at the desk in the corner, as well as other equipment's placed on that desk. The shelves were directly above that desk. Was this what the little girl spirit was referring to? I wondered.

After hearing the little girl's spirit from the first audio evidence report, I opened the second audio (Audio Recording#2). It too was a female. She was saying, "something is going on!" Was this another little girl, or could it have been the little girls' mother from the first audio? My mind was buzzing with different scenarios as to who these people were. Were they from the Barrington family? Maybe they were buried in the cemetery?

The first little girl's whispered words suggested to me that she did recognize that there was something trying to look at them but didn't know what it was called. So, could she have been one of the children that had been buried in the cemetery from the 1800s? Her words also indicate that she is an intelligent spirit, and not a residual one. She was very aware of her surroundings. I think both spirits from audio #1 and audio #2, were fully aware that there were people in the room, "aka, investigators," trying to communicate with something.

The team also caught another female voice that also seemed to be of an intelligent spirit. We will call this audio, female #3. The team is commenting on Momma's house being an older home, and another team member said yeah, and immediately after the team member spoke, you can hear a spirit voice mock the team member by saying, Yeah………

The #4 audio, also female, had some interesting elements in it. The team leader informed me that they would sometimes use trigger items in their investigations to try to communicate with the paranormal. During their setup of the equipment that evening, they had placed a motion-activated Teddy Bear in the kitchen (eating area), but the fascinating thing about this recording, is that the teddy bear had not been turned on yet. At some point during the setup process, 2 of the team members were talking about the teddy bear, and one of the members said, "Hey, we can call it Gangster Boo like they do on Ghost Busters." Both the team members had their recorders on, so they were able to get this amazing recording (audio #1 and audio # 2) of a spirit whispering, "I want Gangster Boo!" This also must be an intelligent spirit due to the ability to comment on the words spoken by the team. Simply chilling.

Audio #5, also female, can be heard humming. This was a little haunting to me because it sounds exactly like my mother. Momma would hum all the time through the house. She had sung in the church choir most of her life and had a beautiful voice. Was she being mimicked by a spirit? Or was this a time warp of my Momma humming some fifty years ago? Whichever it was, that's my mom's voice on that recording.

Audio # 6 is the voice of another female. The voice was picked up from a recorder placed in the Master Bedroom, "my moms' room." You can hear the female voice say, "I know." Not sure what it was in reference to. To me, the words (I know), would be responding words to a question. And the way this voice whispers those words, it does seem like a response to something.

Audio # 7 is the voice of a male. The team is talking about turning *ON* a piece of equipment, and you can hear a spirit's voice say, "ON. "Definitely an intelligent spirit repeating what was said by the team.

Audio # 8 is a male voice.
This audio capture sounds like an exhale or growling.

Hearing all the different voices, they were able to capture, as well as the videos, was quite overwhelming to say the least. And to think from the time of setup to completion, was only around 5 hours. That was 9 different spirits, 9! I can only imagine how many they would have gotten if they had been there all night!

It took weeks for my sister to listen to the audio and watch the videos, she was too afraid she wouldn't be able to sleep after seeing and hearing everything, but after insisting that she watch and listen, she finally agreed to it. I told her this was the only way she would be able to understand what momma and I had lived through, plus she wouldn't be able to deny the things she was seeing or hearing. It would be a Fact.

Dawn started heading for the door as soon as she heard the first voice recording, "NO, NO, NO, I'm out!" she said, throwing up her hands over her head! I said, "No Dawn, you have to listen to them all." After pleading with her to stay, she stood behind me and listened and watched everything. She was quite shaken. Our mother, to this day, has refused to watch any of the audio and video evidence. She did, however, let me read the final written report to her, but that's all. When I asked her why she didn't want to see everything.

"I don't need to," she said," I've already lived it.

16

House For Sale

Momma and I sat in silence for a few minutes after I finished reading the report.

She said, "I am so sorry for all the things you went through in the house when you were growing up. I just didn't understand, I didn't have anything to compare to what you were saying was going on. But now I do, and I am so deeply sorry."

"It's ok, momma," I said.

The following Friday after receiving all the evidence, another one of my nephews had called and talked my mom into going back in the house to get some stuff. She really was afraid to go, but she thought.

"Well, I won't be alone this time, and I can get some more of my important papers."

Haunting of Barrington Heights Estates

So, she and my nephew had the plan that he would pick her up around 9:30 A.M Saturday morning. Dawn and I were not happy about it, but what could we do?

Momma called my nephew early Saturday morning to tell him that she would not be going. She told him she didn't feel well, but the truth was, the spirit that told her about Holly, and that he wouldn't be back for 100 years, had come to her over in the morning, and stood in the doorway of her bedroom of her and Dawn's house and said:

"Don't go back in that house!"

I think he had come back to her to maybe protect her from something tragic that might have occurred that day. We will never know, but Momma took his stern words as a warning.

As Momma, Dawn, and I talked about the house that day just sitting there and the expense of continue paying for lawn service and monthly pool service etc.... and knowing she couldn't stay there anymore, Momma decided to sell the house. She knew it would probably be an investor who would buy it, since all the businesses were popping up everywhere. It sold in 1 month. The person who bought it wasn't planning to do anything with it for a while, and didn't ask about anything like, "is it haunted? or had anyone died in the house? or anything like that." And yes, had the person asked, I would have said yes to the haunted, and NO to any deaths inside the house. It's funny because both houses that I had purchased in my life, the first thing I asked was, "is it haunted? or has anyone died in the house?" That would be a deal-breaker for me right there. I don't care how beautiful it is or what a great deal it may be. That's a BIG HELL NO for this girl!

Momma and I have never been back to the house in Barrington Heights. The last time she or I even looked at the house was the day Drew and I had picked her back up after my doctor's appointment and she was on death's door. With great hesitation, she let the grandkids go up and get what they wanted from my dad's garage, which hadn't been touched since daddy passed. It was full of power tools, and all our childhood bicycles, and lots of vintage items that a collector would love to have. We did warn them about taking items from the house, so they mostly took some pictures.

Think about this for a minute. You have a beautiful home that was built just the way you wanted it.
You had raised your children there and watched your grandchildren as they grew. Enjoyed Sunday dinners almost every week with your family. Every Birthday, Christmas and Holiday was celebrated between those walls. You had a dream inground pool that you even got to watch your great-grandchild enjoy. And as recently as 2018, you had the entire
house completely and beautifully redecorated from top to bottom, and had the kitchen redone just like you had always wanted it to be, only to find yourself at 81 years old, walking away from the house you had called home for 50+ years, a place you had planned to live out the rest of your days. Instead, you're running out the door in fear for your

life with a duffle bag of clothes, and just the clothes on your back! Walking away from EVERYTHING you have ever owned, EVERYTHING you had worked for your entire life! Can you imagine!

I had a friend saying to me, "Well, God's more powerful than bad spirits, and he would have taken care of them." Yes, that is correct, God is almighty, but don't you understand? He did! He moved her away from that. He saved her life. We will let God deal with them since she is gone.

Since we were fearful about bringing any furnishings from the house or her beautiful décor, we hired an estate sale company to come in and sell everything, I mean everything! As the owner of the company walked through each room looking at all her things, Drew came across all the many bibles that Momma had placed all around the house during the time she had demanded the spirits to leave her home. Drew even had one to fall out of the towel closet, which breaks my heart just thinking about how desperate she must have felt to have to put it in with the towels and linens. All her bibles were vintage, and one was her family bible that held the pressed flowers from all her loved ones' funeral; but as hard as it was, she knew the bibles at that point would be a risk to bring into her new residents, since things had escalated after she had placed them in all the rooms, so they too were all left behind.

Mommas' furniture was beautiful, the table in the kitchen area itself was a solid extra-large oak table that had seating for 8, but could fit 10 adults if needed, and if that table were to be purchased today, it would cost over $5000 easily, it sold at auction for $300. Of course, with items sold at an auction, you never know what people are willing to bid, and some of her items only sold for just pennies on the dollars, so, she only ended up with a few thousand dollars for everything after the auctioneer got his cut. Plus, people were starting to get scared of the pandemic coming and that didn't help with sales. But really, it didn't matter at that point, we would have donated everything, because it wasn't coming with us, period!

This should be a good example of why people should be extra careful before bringing used items into their homes from places like antique stores, auctions, goodwill, or thrift stores. I get the reclaim and recycle thing, I really do, but it is a risk you will have to take as to what might come along with that deal. You may get a little more than you bargained for. Just like whoever bought that table for $300, they may have to set an extra plate or two for their extra guest. Or what about the chaise lounge in the sunroom? I have thought on many occasions, "What if some of the spirits had hitched a ride on any of those items?" I hope not! But the truth is, it's very possible.

As Drew and Dawn did the final cleaning of the house before the Closing Date, they only had one more thing to take care of, and that was all the wedding pictures and the hundreds of family photos that the grandkids didn't take; so, they packed them into large boxes and sent them off to a company that would scan them onto a disk, and they had agreed to discard of all the originals for us. We left all our memories behind.

Haunting of Barrington Heights Estates

    We only had 1 or 2 options, 1 was to bury all the pictures on the property so the spirits wouldn't get a chance to escape the estate. I thought as powerful and malicious as some had been, and if any of the spirits wanted to leave, that would have been another perfect transportation route to start a new haunting, since most people would have never left their pictures behind. Remember, we are talking about intelligent spirits; spirits capable of watching your every move and listening to every word spoken, still, since I had already felt their attachment to all the remaining photos, and with the fear of bringing all those bad energies back to where momma would be living, wasn't a risk we were prepared to take. Option 2, have copies made of all the priceless original pictures. It was heartbreaking though, we had to leave all those memories behind, all the pictures that had told the story of our lives; the very proof that we existed on the earth during those years, were now closed away in those brown boxes.

17

My Closing Thoughts

In the beginning of this story, I shared my struggles with writing this book. It was risky, and yet to me, it was important enough to share our family's private experiences, in the hopes that someone can get help before things got to this point. There is hope for you or your loved one that may be experiencing paranormal activity. An option of working with your church may help, or contacting a Paranormal team as we did. There is usually a Paranormal group in every state across the US; just google Paranormal Investigators in your area. If it's just negative energy you have, try sage along with a cleansing prayer might do the trick. If that doesn't work, you may need some help.

Try to find out about the history of the house or apartment etc., you might be surprised by what took place in the very place you call home. Also, ask about the land, "before you buy," ask lots of questions, especially if you are an Empath or Clairvoyant, spirits will seek you out, but if you have these abilities, you probably already know this by now.

And please listen to your children if they start telling you something is bothering them in your home! Young children do not have enough life experience to come up with certain things such as, "There's a man in my room, or something is shaking my bed at night"; and of course, children have imaginations, still, pay close attention to what they are saying and how they are saying it, and not just blow it off as nothing. Do your own investigation and ask the child detailed questions about what they are experiencing and keep a journal of dates and times! If you don't get the answer you are looking for, put a camera in the child's room with a motion detector, this will give you another set of eyes to see what's happening with your child, plus it can send you an alarm to your phone to alert you of any motions it detects.

Also, the same can be true for our senior family members or friends as well. Pay attention without judgment if they should come to you feeling uneasy or feeling something is off in their home; or become worried about unexplainable noises, take the time to listen to their concerns before dismissing it as an age-related delusion. Placing a camera can help answer most questions.

Had I not survived getting my Mechanical Heart/ LVAD in 2016, nobody in my family would have believed my mom's Paranormal encounters. They would have thought she was hallucinating from Parkinson's disease, and I am sure her doctors would have agreed with my family. And Dawn, *"not having any experiences to relate to the paranormal activities occurring in Momma's house,"* "would have put her in a nursing home thinking she was hallucinating from her progressing disease, *"just as most relatives would've done for their loved one's safety."* My mother would be in a nursing home today, or maybe not here at all, if I weren't able to understand what was really happening in that house from my own experiences. And for that reason alone, I will always be grateful. As of May 2021, our mom is still taking her Chemo treatments, and our beloved mother is pampered and loved every moment, just like the beauty queen she has always been.

You might be surprised to know that these events are only one part of my life's stories. I tell people all the time that I have lived a 100 people's lifetime in my short 58 years. My life has been incredibly complicated and yet incredibly blessed all at the same time. I could write so many books about my life, although most people would probably say, NO WAY is it possible that all that SHIT has happened to just 1 person." Well, it did! And since I am on life support, I am going to share these stories as long as I can.

About having to sleep with the lights on since writing this book, ummm yeah, more times than I care to admit.

As hard as it was to write this story mentally, it was also therapeutic. I learned a lot from reliving some of these traumatic experiences and what produced some of the strangest things I do. One of the things that got answered was why I had always slept with my eyes wide opened; now I understand why. I was always afraid to close my eyes growing up, I had to see if anything was coming to hurt me at night. I used to freak my family out because I did that. We were on one of our many camping trips at the beach, I must have been about 10 or 11, and my mother had sent one of our family friends to wake me up for breakfast, and when I didn't show up after they had almost finished eating, my mom asked the friend, "didn't you wake up Raylee Anne?" I told her to come eat, and she was looking straight at me when I said it, the friend replied! Momma just giggled and said, she is asleep, you have to shake her. *"With her eyes opened wide like that!"* the friend questioned Momma. Yep, mom said. The friend was shocked and said she had not seen anything like that before.

Holly Stephen's death is still an unsolved mystery. I did recently get information that the case was going to trial. We would love to know what happened to her and what kind of things or practices were taking place there. As far as the spirit talking about Holly's involvement in the hauntings, I still think he was referring to her because she owned the property, not that she herself was putting a curse on momma, but maybe others on the property were involved in cult type activities that had amped up the spirits that were already there. Or she was just sending momma a warning to protect her. Whatever the case may be, it's sad.

We did talk to Ray and his wife again after momma moved, we had known that they had suspected they had paranormal activity too, but Ray's wife finally did tell me it was a little more than that; they too had a bad spirit in their home, and that many years ago when her daughter was growing up, a malevolent spirit had attacked her too, and had told her daughter it was going to kill her. Could it be some of the same spirits we had? I would have to say a resounding yes since momma and Ray's property were side by side.

I suspect from all the information that I have been able to retrieve, including some obituaries of the Barrington family, that most of the graves were never relocated to a new cemetery. Some would have been from the 1800s, so the bodies most likely would have been buried in a wooden coffin, and I would think it is safe to say that by the 1950s and 1960s, everything, including the wooden box coffin, would have returned to dusk leaving nothing to take. I am sure many souls were left in that cemetery, and upon some latest information, I think it's an 80% chance that part of the cemetery was located on my mother's property as well. Another high possibility is that the Stephens, along with Ray's property, were most likely part owners of this most haunted cemetery too. I learned that the Barrington family had some of their family in the military, as well as out-of-state relatives, sent to the cemetery for their burials in the 1800s.

Upon my research on how families relocated old family cemeteries, I learned that it is very costly to relocate a family loved one to a different site, so most families just put a new headstone or marker up at the new location as a memorial for their deceased family member. That, in my opinion, might explain why the family may have decided to just pile up the grave headstones and markers, and leave them behind. If this did happen in this case, the old heavy grave markers would not be of any value anymore. Because who would take the bodies and leave the headstone? How would you know what gravestone belonged to whosever's body if the markers were left in a pile? We will never know all the answers or just how many were buried there or relocated from there.

My mother used to tell me, "Ghost can't hurt you!" when I was a little girl being tormented constantly.

Momma has changed her mind ....

The End

Look for the pages at the front of this book for the **"Evidence Links for YouTubes"** The Haunting of Barrington Heights Estates." You will be able to see and hear the actual evidence collected at the time of the investigation, as well as the actual recording of the Hispanic music described in the book. I have included a slideshow from the security camera of the actual ladies that I had described as the "Voodoo Ladies" in the book. Also, I wanted to share some personal pictures I took on a vacation in October 2011 in Venice. It is of a Time Warp of Soldiers in a Gondola as well the Gondolier driving the boat. I caught this a few minutes after passing St Mark's Square, as I was walking toward the bridge. That's where I noticed these amazing lights coming out of the sky beside a building and the bridge and I knew right away they were of a Paranormal nature or something unworldly, so I took a couple of pictures. Boy, was I right! I will put this in a slideshow ……...

I will also have the actual report from the investigation for you to view.

Also, you can see these Videos and Audios at

@rayleeanne1 on TikTok

Also, please follow us on Facebook. I would love to chat with y'all and get your thoughts about the book.

The Haunting of Barrington Heights Estates.

Haunting of Barrington Heights Estates

Copy of The Final Report From The Investigation

Case: SC

Lead: Shaun **Investigators:**

Sabrina, Tori, Michael, Sandy, Tammy, and O
Date: November 23, 2019

EVP Session #1

Living Room: Sabrina & Sandy
Front left bedroom: Tammy & Michael
Back right bedroom: Tori & O

EVP Session #2

Sunroom: Tori & Sandy
Dining Room: Tammy & Sabina
Back Left bedroom: Michael & O

EVP Session #3

Living Room: Tammy & O
Front left bedroom: Sabrina & Tori
Back right bedroom: Michael & Sandy

Spirit Box Session

Living Room: All Investigators

Report by Shaun E.

Initial impression:

Single story house on dead-end road. 3 other buildings on the property. Quiet neighborhood. Vehicle traffic could be heard from behind the home.

Investigation:

Clients were not in the home and SCPRAI investigated by ourselves.

As lead, I paired the Investigators into 3 teams of 2. I monitored the DVR for the investigation. Captured Multiple possible EVP (Electronic Voice Phenomena) with digital recorder. Those will be Labeled SC Two DVR recordings in the front left bedroom of the 360° ParaScope (Triboelectric Field Meter- Follows static electricity fields horizontally, allowing Investigators to be informed of the direction the field is traveling). The device was placed on the stand next to the door by the left side closet. I'm sending a video of the hallway at the same time of both.

In the first video from the hallway, I am seen walking toward the bedroom. On the video from the bedroom, the Periscope activates, but the direction of static electricity is moving away from me. As if something is walking away as I walk towards the room.

In the second video from the hallway, investigators are seen in the hallway, but move to the kitchen. The ParaScope activates again, but this time in the direction towards the door. As if something is walking back towards the door. Possibly to look out at us. Just to be clear, this is only speculation. There is no explanation why static electricity would generate in that area, or why it's moving.

As a team, we walked around outside, checking the other buildings. Other investigators began to feel ill. After walking by the open-face garage, I discovered ants all over my legs and shoes.

Closing Impression

No personal experiences other than the feeling of being watched. With the evidence gathered, and other investigators feeling ill or drained, a future investigation and cleansing may be needed.

Report by Tammy M.

Initial Impression

Brick house on a dead end. One neighbor to the left. Trees across the road.

Walk-in Impression

When I first walked in, I felt as if I should not be there. It could have been it being my first investigation and being in someone's house that I did not know, but as the evening went on, the feeling did not let up, but was most intense in the living room and hallway. The dining room was small yet felt larger than it was. I did not have any of this oppressive feeling outside of the house anywhere on the property. I did, however, have a very strong repulsive feeling directed towards the desk in the corner of the living room. Even though after a time, the heavy feeling faded, it persisted near the desk in the corner.

Bedroom 1 – Closets

Michael and I started in the first bedroom with reported activity centered around the closets. Michael sat on the floor at the foot of the bed, I sat on the bed itself. The 360 Parascope was sitting on a side table in front of one of the closets. I had a digital recorder, and I sat my K2 meter on the bed away from me. Michael and I asked a few questions and then conversed, occasionally stopping to ask questions. At one point, the 360 lit up on the side facing towards the wall/flower arrangement. At the same time, my K2 meter began to flash all the way into the red. The 360 slowly began to light upon the side towards the closet, until it was lit up 180 degrees from where it had started. All during this time, we asked questions and the K2 meter flashed. All of this happened within 5-6 minutes.

Dining Room

Sabrina and I walked into the dining room and shut the door. It didn't have a negative oppressive feeling, but a comfortable one. We both remarked on how the room felt larger than it was. I stood on one side of the table with my back to the window, Sabrina was across the table with her back to the wall. I placed my digital recorder on one end of the table and Sabrina place the K2 meter on the opposite end. We began by asking questions and then turned to the conversation. At one point, I noticed a subtle, yet obvious lighting in the room. I first thought either a security light had turned on outside, or someone else walked outside and turned a flashlight on. I immediately turned around to look outside – the blinds were open- but there were no outside lights on other that the streetlight that had been on the entire time, nor was there anyone outside. I continued to face the window while Sabrina and I asked questions. After a few minutes, I turned back to face Sabrina. Shortly thereafter, Sabrina exclaimed to have seen a light among a grouping of photographs that were sitting on a table in the corner. We both agreed to make note of what we had seen, but to wait until the group got together to talk about experiences before revealing what we had seen.

Living Room

O. and I sat in the living room. I had placed an IR camera and a GoPro directed towards the desk in the corner. I sat a Data Logger on the corner of the desk itself. When I stood by the desk, I had an overwhelming feeling that I did not need to be there. There were also two K2 meters both set where cameras could record activity. I sat my digital recorder on the floor beside me and began by asking questions. Shaun, joined in at that point. Neither K2 went off, nor did the Data Logger other than what would be a normal shift in temperature – less than one degree.

Closing Impression

I do feel there is something in the house, not so much outside. It was revealed that there was a small family cemetery across the road from the house and the homeowners had been told that the remains had been relocated, but the headstones were left intact. This is not normally the case unless the markers are historic in nature.

I do agree with the neighbors that the bodies have not been removed and may be a factor. I think research into the prior family, property and the deceased would be a good idea.

Possible EVP attached. Recorded during equipment setup and is oddly clear but does not follow conversation.

Report By Sabrina C.

Initial impression:

As I pulled up, the house was an older ranch style, nice. A large yard with 3 buildings and an in-ground pool. The home is at the end of the neighborhood road, the area nice and seemingly quiet.

First impression walking into the home:

Not too uncomfortable walking into the first room, the living room. The home was kept and neat. During the initial walk through inside of the home, I became uneasy when walking into the front bedroom, all other rooms were comfortable upon the first impression. A group of us walked the parameters of the yard shortly after we arrived. Upon walking the parameters, we walked near the building that is also garage, to the right of the pool. When I approached this building, I had a severe pain in the temporal area of my head. This pain was strong enough to stop me for a minute and grab my head. I let my partner know what was going on with my head and that I needed just a minute to gather myself. There was also two more team members that were walking the parameter well. Tori, who was one of those two, had the same experience in the same exact spot of the yard that I did. Besides that building. Pain to the head.

Upon continuing to walk the perimeter of the yard, we walked up on the porch where there was a statue of a large dog... in the area with this statue, feelings of peacefulness seemed to surround that area.

Living Room

My first impression when walking into the living room when I first arrived of not being too uncomfortable faded when we went in there to investigate. I sat on the floor near a recliner and immediately began to feel a sensation of nausea and an unknown presence, and an immediate need to move to a different area of the room. After being in there for just a while, I picked up the EMF meter and began to ask general questions. These questions had replying to spikes on the EMF meter. Spikes when I would ask a question as well as no movement on the meter when I would request that whenever was responding to me, not respond. This was consistent for several minutes before growing quiet. There was also several minutes that the room seemed to get "lighter" as if the sun were in a setting phase, eventually remaining dark.

Dining Room

The 2nd room I went into was the dining room. While in there, I did not feel uncomfortable, however, there was a small light that appeared in betwixt and between several pictures that were displayed on a table in the corner of the room, for about 15 seconds. My partner also mentioned of the wall behind me, which would have been the wall closest to the hall, becoming brighter as if a car was passing by and the headlights were to shine into the house and against that wall.

Bedroom 1 – Closets

There was not much discomfort or feelings of being uneasy throughout the other rooms that I investigated, aside from the front bedroom. The front bedroom was the final room that I investigated with my partner. As she and I were in that room, we both felt an uneasiness. As well as I discovered, I had a knot on my head, possibly from the pain earlier felt when outside as it was in the area of pain. No other experiences while in there.

Outside

After this, the full team met back in the kitchen to discuss the next steps of going outside as the full team. I went to the bathroom that was closest to the living room before heading outside and was very uncomfortable in there and felt like I had to get out of that bathroom asap. Once we headed outside, we walked to an overgrown area of the house that is located across the road where cars were parked then towards the back yard.

When walking back towards the back yard, we walked towards the building that I had head pain when initially walking beside it. As we approached and walked through that same area, again, I had a sharp pain in my head as well as the team member who had the head pain during the initial parameter walk. I as well as a few others, had gotten ants, from somewhere in the yard, that got all over our feet and legs.

Closing Impression

I seemed to keep that heightened pain in my head until leaving the property that evening and felt something possibly attached to me and asked for cleansing. I did not have any findings from my recordings or photos, however I had several personal experiences, as well as other team members obtained evidence with their personal experiences as well as recordings.

Report By Tori

First impressions:

- Feelings of being watched and caution before going to the location
- Feelings of being unwelcome and heaviness upon stepping on the property
- Large, ranch style home with a spacious backyard
- Feelings of pressure on my head, nausea, and being drained of energy upon entering the house

Personal Experience/Evidence:

- Felt like I was hit in the back of the head that lasted through the next day.
- While on the property, I didn't directly communicate with what was there until the cleansing. I don't know why but I feel like it was to protect myself.
- Upon entering the gazebo outside the house, the area through the windows was darker than it was on the outside of the structure.

- Captured a few inaudible EVPs that came from the living room/ kitchen area.
- Captured an EVP saying "Gangster Boo" after speaking about it with another investigator in the kitchen/dining room area.
- Captured an EVP saying "I know" in the master bedroom while no one was in the room at the time.
- During the cleansing, it felt like I was having to add more energy and focus more than during other cleansings.
- Leaving the property, I was feeling drained, confused, and just not myself for the next couple of days.

Final Impressions:

- There is activity at the location that cannot be debunked or explained outright. It is unknown at this time if it is related to the possible graves across the road, a possible curse on the homeowner, or if it is related to something else. I feel more investigation is needed to determine the origin of the activity. I do also feel that another cleansing will be needed on the property to help get rid of activity.

Shaun E.
-Board Member
-Lead Investigator
-Tech Support/Website Admin
South Carolina Paranormal Research and Investigations

Haunting of Barrington Heights Estates

Made in the USA
Columbia, SC
19 March 2023